The

CYBER
Spellbook

MAGICK *in the* VIRTUAL WORLD

By

SIRONA KNIGHT

and

PATRICIA TELESCO

NEW PAGE BOOKS
A division of The Career Press, Inc.
Franklin Lakes, NJ

THE CYBER SPELLBOOK: MAGICK IN THE VIRTUAL WORLD
Edited by Kate Preston
Typeset by Eileen Dow Munson
Cover design by Diane Y. Chin
Printed in the U.S.A. by Book-mart Press

To order this title, please call toll-free 1-800-CAREER-1 (NJ and Canada: 201-848-0310) to order using VISA or MasterCard, or for further information on books from Career Press.

The Career Press, Inc., 3 Tice Road, PO Box 687,
Franklin Lakes, NJ 07417
www.careerpress.com
www.newpagebooks.com

Library of Congress Cataloging-in-Publication Data
Knight, Sirona, 1955-
    The cyber spellbook : magick in the virtual world / by Sirona Knight and Patricia Telesco.
        p. cm.
    Includes bibliographical references (p.) and index.
    1. Witchcraft. 2. Virtual reality. 3. Cyberspace. I. Knight, Sirona, 1955- II. Title.

BF1571 .T425 2002
133.4'3—dc21

                                                2002025508

Sirona would like to dedicate this book to one of our founding fathers,
Benjamin Franklin,
to Nicola Telsa, the genius who discovered alternating current,
and to Ron Fry, her bold and visionary publisher.

Trish would like to dedicate this book to her computer (fondly named Serek)
and her husband, who is to thank for making her the cyber-geekette she is today.

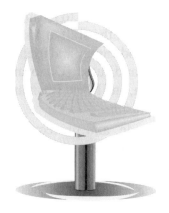

Acknowledgments

Many people encouraged and helped me to give this book legs, and I am grateful to all of you. Loving and hugging thanks to my family and friends, especially Michael, my husband, Sky, our son, and my parents. I would like to acknowledge Mike Lewis for his friendship, insight ,and continued faith in my writing. Blessings and loving thanks to my co-author, Trish Telesco, without whom this book could have never been written. You rock Lady! Also, I would like to thank Lisa Hagan at Paraview. Many heartfelt thank to Stacey Farkas and Kate Preston for their enthusiasm, expertise, and superb editing job. I thank my lucky stars and sincerely appreciate all of the bright, forward-thinking people at New Page Books including Anne Brooks, Karen Wolf, Laurie Kelly, Kirsten Beucler, Brianna Rosen, Jackie Michaels, Jenny Crespo, and Georgio Simeon. Thank you for being such a joy to work with!

I would like to extend a special thank you to everyone at *Magical Blend Magazine*, especially author and publisher, Michael Peter Langevin, for his continued support,

Philosophy, Ethics, and Practices of Cyber Witches

> "Societies will, of course, wish to exercise
> prudence in deciding which technologies, that
> is, which applications of science are to be
> pursued and which not. But without funding
> basic research, without supporting the
> acquisition of knowledge for its own sake, our
> options become dangerously limited."
>
> —Carl Sagan

Catching the Cyber Wave

It is indeed a brave new world in which we live. All around us situations and technologies transform at warp speeds, leaving many people—even the most stalwart Neo-Pagan and Witch—completely out of breath. There are times when we think we are all just trying to keep up, yet by the time we think we've caught the wave, we're already outdated!

One of the fantastic things about being Cyber Witches is that it helps us catch that wave, and also ride it as long and as far as it will take us. Similar to what's expressed in Mr. Sagan's visionary words, today we Witches want to expand our wisdom and are not content with limits. Nor are we comfortable with the idea of foregoing our magickal growth by complacently relying only on those things recommended by our ancestors or those dictated by custom.

First, our forebears never anticipated all the conveniences we have now. Most of us wouldn't have believed them to be possible as little as 20 years ago. What we do know, however, is that if our forebearers had possessed such items, the gadgets would have been put to good use in every aspect of life. Even up to 100 years ago folks were pragmatic. They didn't buy, grow, or make something unless it had numerous applications!

Second, Witches and Neo-Pagans feel strongly that spiritual pursuits must grow and transform with society, self, and even on a grander scale, the Universe. Without ongoing innovation the power of our Path fades into dogma. With this in mind, Cyber Magick becomes very important to our future. It builds a two-way bridge that honors our history and spans into the future with a hopeful on-ramp. Now you have a chance to help build and tend that bridge by applying the philosophy, ethics, and practices of this Path to your own, or by making it *your* Path.

Philosophy and Cyber Ethics

The Path of the Cyber Witch can be either philosophical or religious depending on a person's perspective. A philosophy is a way of thinking and a way of looking at the world. Philosophy seeks wisdom then acts accordingly. A religion is similar, but has elements of faith that guide both thought and action. Cyber Witches can choose either a religious position or a philosophical position and apply it equally well to magick, because magick is basically neutral. The energy it creates can be positive or negative. The intent and ethics that drive the energy lie solely in the hands of the wielder. It's important to use your energy wisely.

The Cyber Witch's philosophy, in its simplest form, is a combination of metaphysics, ecology, alchemy, technology, integrity, humor, and old-fashioned human innovation. The metaphysical part of the equation is self-explanatory. We apply magickal arts and energy to our all efforts (both temporal and spiritual), in rather new and interesting ways. The Cyber Witch's spiritual pursuits and daily reality are one. In fact, one of the goals for Cyber Witchery is to become the magick in word and deed, 24 hours a day, seven days a week. By so doing, we begin transforming our reality, and positively effecting everyone and everything our lives touch.

This may sound too grand for any one person, but it isn't. One thing that Cyber Witches know, beyond any doubt, is that one person with willful focus and a heart intent on working for the good of all *can* make a difference. Sometimes that difference is something big, but more often it comes in small daily gestures. While the big stuff is nice (and certainly sustains our faith), the daily walking of our Path is what builds long-term, strong foundations. And, like it or not, even in magick some things take time. Quality living is rarely something that happens overnight or without effort.

Ecologically, the Cyber Witch does not believe in the old concept of humans having dominion over the Earth. Neo-Pagans as a whole have a partnership with Nature and natural laws. No matter where we may be, or how technically aligned our Path, we should be mindful of our responsibility to this planet and use its gifts wisely.

Globally this ecological focus boils down to keeping humankind off the endangered species list. Personally it means that even though you, the Cyber Witch, live amidst the concrete jungle, surrounded by technological devices, you continue your connection with the Mother. Having that connection is even more sacred because it provides balance and spiritual symmetry.

Make no mistake about it, honoring that connection can get a little tricky. Remember that underneath all the pavement, earth is still there. She's still vital and certainly still trying to speak to our hearts. We just need to regularly slow down enough to really listen!

Alchemically, the Cyber Witch resonates with the need for transformation. The ancient alchemists concerned themselves chiefly with taking ordinary metal and turning it into gold. In similar fashion, Cyber Witches take the metal of our daily life and transform it into the gold of magick and a progressive spiritual Path. Akin to a chemical reaction, we spiritually react to the changes in our society, culture, and personal experiences with appropriate alterations of our own. In this manner, our magickal practices and ideals will never suffer becoming outmoded or antiquated. If anything, they have visionary potential.

It bears mentioning that the continual "tweaking" doesn't just affect outward things. It's something that touches the Cyber Witch's very soul. Our thoughts and understanding grow, our bodies become a temple, and our spirits blossom in that sacred space. Because magick is to turn and change, and *we* are the magick, this makes perfect sense!

Technology is the fun part of this Path, but also perhaps the most challenging. As previously mentioned, the Cyber

Witch considers everything in life as having metaphysical potential. Nonetheless, even the most proficient Techno-Pagan sometimes has trouble viewing a slab of plastic, a bundle of wires, or a piece of synthetic fabric as remotely spiritual.

The key to the successful application of technology is perspective. Rather than looking superficially, pause for a moment and consider the symbolic value of an item based on the way you use it every day. Just 100 years ago a farmer might have considered a hoe a suitable tool for weeding out a troublemaker, or perhaps could have used it as a makeshift wand. Similarly, the Cyber Witch looks at a cell phone and sees it as a potential implement for communication spells, or perhaps travel-oriented magick because we typically use cell phones while we're traveling!

As you can see, there is little difference in Cyber Witch, but for the temporal setting and objects available. Unfortunately, there is a tendency in our society to say, "What you see is what you get." Many times you don't stop to look past the surface potential of things just because you're not brought up that way.

Once you begin to open your mind to the possibilities, however, you'll never be able to go through a supermarket or office supply store in the same manner. Suddenly everything takes on metaphoric value for spells and rituals. A calculator, for example, screams of the conscious mind, weighing options, financial bottom lines, and could even become a tool for divination. A can opener, by comparison, seems to talk of opportunities, uncovering hidden matters, and releasing specific types of energy into one's life. See how easy that is? It all makes perfect sense because the way we use these items already implies a symbolic value. We'll be talking more about specific components in Chapter 3, but for now let that concept settle in a bit.

Cyber Witch Integrity

Next we come to integrity. Responsibility and mores are important to Cyber Witches. This is not a "rules-be-damned" approach to life or magick. Cyber Witches recognized that all things (both in and out of cyberspace) are connected. What we do magickally can affect so much more than self or the situations in our lives that it should not be undertaken without proper forethought and consideration. Before any type of magick comes into play, Cyber Witches ask themselves simple questions such as:

❋ Could I accomplish this through normal means? If so, why am I using magick?

❋ Am I in the right frame of mind to work a spell or ritual?

❋ What's the motivation here? Is this for the good of all?

❋ Have I considered the potential outcomes of this working fully, and prepared it properly so it harms none?

❋ Does anything about this process bother me ethically or nag at my higher senses?

❋ Can this process be altered so it's more personally meaningful and so it better reflects my Path?

❋ Is this process Earth-friendly?

These kinds of questions are what set any honest Witch or Neo-Pagan apart from those who abuse magick for personal gratification and ego. Witches are people, too, and that means even the most adept practitioner is prone to human failings.

Taking time out before enacting magick to truly internalize the breadth of what you're about to undertake will help you avoid a number of the vanity-oriented pitfalls.

When reading the previous questions, you'll notice that the first one is very important to cyber integrity. We already know that quality magickal living rarely happens without a little elbow grease. The authors of this book both advocate honest effort in practicing great magick. If you can do it yourself, do so. If you want to support a goal magickally, still be ready to work for that goal mundanely. Putting it quite simply: If you are not willing to put some viable effort into your metaphysical goals, you're giving up your role as a co-creator. This is your life, your reality, and your magick. It's worth investing your effort.

Innovation, Cunning, and Humor

Without innovation, this book wouldn't exist. A very long time ago, someone, somewhere, rummaged around in the soil, gathered an herb, a rock, and a feather and made an amulet. A little later, another person, elsewhere, put together a verbal charm to invite positive energy into his or her life. Later still, someone devised the first ritual, drew the first Magick Circle, and donned garb suited to his or her sacred position. All of these stages in magick represent innovation and transmutation. Each person trusted fully in the power he or she was creating; each worked according to cultural symbols and prevalent knowledge. The Cyber Witch embraces that legacy and says it's time to evolve again.

We gather up the figurative gene pool of technology and celebrate all that it can become substantively and magickally with a little imagination. To that pool of information and human-made contrivances we add our personal vision, any desired cultural or societal overtones, and life experiences to create something truly meaningful and potent. This blend responds to tradition by using successful constructs and by honoring the historical Witch's cleverness. That is why we were called *cunning* folk! The blend also responds to the here and now by making sense of the new symbolic input that barrages our senses every day—the cyber world.

Speaking of senses and sensibility, a good sense of humor is essential to any spiritual path. Let's face it; everyday life presents challenges before you become a Witch, let alone thereafter. It isn't always rosy or fun, but humor makes even the worst of moments a little easier to bear.

Cyber Witches know that laughter has very real power. It breaks up negativity. If you've ever watched someone with the giggles, you've seen how it becomes contagious. Laughter creates its own cone of power that can be directed by a well-trained metaphysician.

There is very little about cyber spellcraft and ritual that's maudlin or boring. Cyber Witches strive to live life to its fullest, so they work and play hard. Part of that frolicsome spirit comes out in the way they devise their magick. Here puns are welcomed and encouraged. Also, it requires a humorous approach to technological "doohickies" to begin really seeing their spiritual potential. For example, people giggle at Trish when they see an old memory card on her key chain. Nonetheless, for her it's akin to tying a string around her finger. The memory card helps her "recall" and the humor in the visual pun just gives more energy to this little charm.

Finally, and most importantly, the Cyber Witch's philosophy responds to the future by thinking and looking forward. We will avoid stagnating or getting stuck in mire because we're already riding a virtual wave to the shore of enlightenment. What we plant today with innovation will bloom and grow, manifesting in our very souls. The seeds harvested from that potent magickal philosophy can then be cultivated by future generations.

Cyber Witch Practices

Now that we've examined the basic ideology behind Cyber Craft, the next obvious question becomes—what exactly do Cyber Witches do? That question is not easily answered. Because Cyber Craft depends heavily on the individual's ability to "wing it" as well as personal insight, the ways in which the Cyber Witch practices and celebrates the Craft can be as unique as each individual walking the Path. The eclectic, vision-oriented nature of Witchery is very important to this overall Path.

Having said that, Cyber Witches do have some white, black, and gray outlines to which they bring their proverbial crayons. Those outlines consist of the traditional methods Witches have been using successfully for decades, if not eons. Included in this list we find spellcasting, charm and amulet creation, meditation, ritual work, shapeshifting, visualization, prayer, and sympathetic magick, all of which are means of gathering energy and redirecting it toward a specific goal.

Most of you have at least a little exposure to magickal traditions and Witchery, but just in case, we'd like to take a moment to define each of these methods. We would also like to provide examples as they apply specifically to Cyber Craft. This information will help you understand the constructs used later in this book, as well as give you the means to personalize those methods, if desired.

Spellcasting is one of the most popular procedures in the Witch's kit. Some spells require nothing more than the Witch's will and a few words or thoughts to activate the energy. Other spells are far more complicated. That complexity derives from the supportive measures recommended by the spell's instructions. What exactly constitutes a supportive measure? Quite simply, it's anything that the Witch feels enhances his or her focus, improves magickal precision as the pattern unfolds to the universe, and increases the amount of manifesting power. Supportive measures include:

* Casting the spell during auspicious astrological times or lunar phases.

* Using specially blessed and cleansed components (some of which might also have to be gathered at specific times).

* Repeating the spell over a set number of days, weeks, or even months.

* Enacting the spell within a properly cast Magick Circle or other special location.

* Adding incantations or prayers.

* Adding gestures, actions, and movements at specific moments in the spell (such as raising arms outward to direct the energy outward upon casting).

* Adding other sensory cues to the workspace, each of which is chosen for its symbolic value (the more senses you use in spellcraft the greater the chances become of accurate, positive manifestation).

Many people have asked us whether a more complex spell raises more power. That depends very much on the Cyber Witch. If you're someone who can recite a magickal ditty with a strongly focused will and firm convictions, that can easily manifest just as potently into a complicated process that distracts you with all the associated bells and whistles. On the other hand, someone who enjoys ritual and the gradual building of power (which often improves said person's focus) will often find a complex approach works better.

The difference between folk magick and ritual or High Magick is dramatic from an observer's standpoint, but not that different in overall results if you trust the process. Therefore a key rule in Cyber Craft is know yourself. Don't try to walk in anyone else's cyber shoes! You are your own cyber priestess or priest. Only you can determine which approach is best or works best for you.

Cyber Charms, Amulets, Talismans, and Fetishes

Jumping off the soapbox, let's move on to charms, amulets, talismans, and fetishes. These items act as mini-spells housed in an object or a combination of objects, all of which are easily portable. They get their power from a combination of symbolic value ascribed to the item(s) and the energizing provided by the Witch.

We've already talked briefly about discerning the symbolic value of any item (be it natural or human-made). Just to recap, you can depend upon a traditional correspondence list if you have one handy, or just trust your instincts. What's most important is that the symbolism *you* see in an item matches that of your magick. Energizing takes many forms. For example, the Witch might put spell components in direct sunlight or moonlight for a specific amount of time. Sunlight promotes active energy and supports goals relating to the conscious mind. Moonlight strengthens receptive energies and promotes goals relating to the superconscious or subconscious mind. You can refer to Chapter 3 (under Care and Keeping of Cyber Components) for more information and ideas on energizing.

Typical base components for charms include metals, stones, plant matter, fabric, candle wax, pins, fruit, coins, and anything else that has the appropriate symbolic value. To this list the Cyber Witch adds just about everything you can find in your junk drawer at home. Here's just a small sampling:

✳ Staples.

✳ AAA batteries.

✳ Tea candles.

✳ Paper clips.

✳ Erasers (various colors).

✳ Glue sticks.

✳ Screws and nails.

✳ Crayons.

✳ Duct tape and electrical tape.

✳ White-Out.

✳ Mailing labels.

✳ Canned air.

✳ Phone and computer cables and connectors.

✳ Rubber bands.

✳ Screwdriver.

✳ Scissors.

✳ Lighters and matches.

As was the case with spells, charms, amulets, fetishes, and talisman, creation can be simple or it can become very complex. A simple illustration was Trish's memory card charm. All it required was punching a hole in the card and empowering it with an incantation recited four times (four is the number of foundations). On the other hand, many magickal treatises have painstaking, exacting details that must be followed for the resulting charm or amulet to be effective. Among these details we sometimes find taboos for the magi. She or he might have to abstain from food or sexual activity for a period of time beforehand, for example. Theoretically this abstention helped purify one's spirit so the magick would manifest accurately (without worldly taint).

Cyber Witches can certainly consider that kind of abstention as an offering and a way to cleans their auras if they choose (and if it's physically safe). However, when you're in a pinch for time it may be just as easy to take a shower or wash your hands. Both actions imply order and wholesomeness. The only difference is that now you'll be directing intention into the action and approaching it as a sacred act.

Cyber Meditation and Visualization

Meditation and visualization often go hand in hand. Meditation teaches you how to still your spirit and direct your mind toward one task or concept. This singularity of mind is very important magickally because you need to keep your energy from scattering. Visualization helps by providing something on which to focus your attention and will. Deep breathing and relaxation methods also frequently play an important role in the success or failure of both processes. Both of these working in tandem with the meditation help you move past the self and the now and into that world between the worlds where magick resides.

It's in the visualization part of the equation that Cyber Witchery really shines. Although, a more traditional Witch may use the image of a tranquil, natural location to quell anger, the Cyber Witch might visualize himself or herself in front of the air conditioner, cooling off and chilling out!

How does technology figure into meditation and visualization? Cyber Witches like to play music or listen to natural sounds emanating from their computer, stereo, or CD player to set the mood. This background ambiance needs to be kept at a level that helps maintain focus as opposed to being a distraction. Trish likes very quiet music when she meditates, but someone with noisy neighbors might want to crank it up so the outside world isn't so intrusive.

Another modern addition to meditation (or rituals, for that matter) is that of a plug-in aromatic. Just before starting the meditation, pick an aroma that matches the overall focus of your effort and put it into the specialized container in a nearby wall outlet. This literally turns on that scent's energy!

Cyber Ritual

By definition, a ritual is anything we repeat with spiritual overtones. Using that framework, Trish knows that her morning cup of coffee is a ritual just as Sirona's cup of chamomile tea is her morning ritual! This kind of reverence, although humorous, is important. Cyber Witches recognize that life itself is a sacred act. It is a ritual where we become a vessel and a tool if we allow ourselves to.

Typically, ritual takes place within the protective sphere of a fully erected Magick Circle. We'll go into creating sacred space more specifically in Chapter 2, but please realize that not all situations necessitate this kind of magickal warding.

The Cyber Witch is typically very pragmatic. If the individual is working a short, simple ritual, the time and effort necessary to call in the Quarters may not make sense. So instead, he or she will acknowledge the sacred space of self or activate pre-prepared wards in and around their home.

Whether or not the ritual includes a Magick Circle isn't what sets cyber rituals apart. It's the tools used within that space. Now rather than (or in addition to) traditional Quarter markings and altar regalia we might find a plethora of other objects. For example, it's not unusual to find a blue candle or a seashell in the west to represent the Element of Water. The Cyber Witch, however, might substitute a faucet that resides in that direction so he or she can literally "turn on" Water's energy as they invoke that Quarter. Instead of a feather for Air, he or she might have an electric fan!

What about outdoor rituals, you ask? Well, now instead of the faucet how about a handy hose or squirt gun? For the electric fan, there are now small, battery-operated substitutes. You can see how this whole process can be a great deal of fun, and an exercise in stretching one's perceptions and being more aware of everything in your environment, whatever that environment may be.

So where does prayer work into this rather free-wheeling, fly-by-your-broomstick structure of Cyber Witchery? The same place it does in any tradition. Prayer is a way that we commune with Spirit, and a time in which we also heed that Divine voice. The word talk implies communication, and that means both speaking and listening

Whether you imagine Spirit to be the spark of the big bang, Buddha, or Goddess and God, matters little. What matters is the communication. What matters is opening oneself to those sacred energies and honoring them regularly. For Cyber Witches, this may be doubly important again because of the heavy role human invention and technology plays in their Path. That spiritual balance keeps our magick from drying up. It also keeps us from becoming too mechanistic.

Sympathetic Cyber Magick

Finally we come to the idea of sympathetic magick. Now, it's true that sympathy and the Law of Signatures play a role in all of the aforementioned methods, but for the Cyber Witch it becomes a key ingredient. The idea of sympathy states that a properly utilized symbolic item will act on what that item represents over large spaces (the Internet is about as large a space as can be conceived!). In fact, in a sacred context, a symbol is just as powerful as what it represents. There is no differentiation.

The Law of Signatures goes on to say that everything in Nature has a shape, color, or other signifier that implies its proper use. Cyber Witches take a little liberty with this law, and add a twist. Now everything that is made by humans also has a pattern that can imply function, but only if you respect it and approach it with the right attitude in your heart and spirit.

So if all of that, bundled up in a neat computer cable with a bow, seems appealing—you too can be a Cyber Witch! The first step along this Path is deciding what you want to do and giving it a whirl. The rest of this book will help you do that.

Cyber Witch Rite of Self-Dedication

For those new to the Path of magick, it's always nice to set aside a moment to honor your choice to practice and welcome those energies into your life and home. The Cyber Rite of

Self-Dedication explains how to do this using technology as a partner in the process. Note that this is a dedication and a personal and private commitment between you and the Divine. It is *not* an initiation, because the word initiation implies some type of group acceptance or training. Even so, it isn't something entered lightly.

Before embarking on a cyber self-dedication, we recommend you spend at least a few days in prayer or meditation. A weekend might be best, or a span where you don't have to be interrupted by work and other responsibilities. Basically these couple of days act as a touchstone—a time to reflect on where you've come from and where you hope to go. It's also a chance to make sure this is the right Path and choice for you.

What You Will Need

Sliced lemon, lavender flowers, gauze cloth, special clothing, anointing oil (your choice of aroma, but lotus is good for promoting spirituality), three candles (one for the old self, one for the new, and one for Spirit), your favorite magickal tools (especially those that are technologically oriented), a bowl of flower petals (any), and a blank book or disk to keep a record of your reflections on this moment.

Note: Everything but the herbs and clothing go on your altar. The other two items are for the ritual bath.

Location

The Cyber Witch's home is her or his castle, and that's also where most of us keep all our magickal implements, so we suggest working at home in the room where you perform most spiritual functions. You will, however, need to have a window handy.

Personal Preparation

Take a long relaxing bath in water into which you've added some sliced lemon and lavender flowers bundled in a gauze cloth. Lemon purifies. Lavender promotes peace with your decision. As you get out of the tub try to leave behind tensions, worries, and any thoughts of the mundane world. Release them to the water, then pick up the outfit you've chosen and clothe yourself in magick.

In the Sacred Space

Light the candle that represents the old self, then begin your invocation in the East, the direction of new beginnings. (Note: If you have implements that honor and represent the Quarters, they should be put out in their proper location before the invocation). Walk clockwise, stopping at each directional Quarter, as you say,

> Guardians of the East and Air,
>
> I call and charge you.
>
> Come and witness this rite,
>
> My dedication to Cyber Magick.
>
> Grant me a new mind and perspective
>
> To walk this Path in truth and beauty.

Face South and say,

> Guardians of the South and Fire,
>
> I call and charge you.
>
> Come and witness this spiritual spark
>
> And keep it burning.

Grant me the passion and playfulness

With which to embark on this new life.

Face West and say,

Guardians of the West and Water,

I call and charge you.

Come and witness this, my heart's desire

To practice Cyber Craft.

Grant me the creativity

With which to work my magickal arts.

Face North and say,

Guardians of the North and Earth,

I call and charge you.

Come and witness this, the first sprouting of the tree

Which is my spirit.

Grant me strong roots so that I may proceed

Confidently on the Path of Cyber Craft.

Move to your altar and say,

Spirit, I light your candle on my altar

And it also burns in my heart.

Witness my dedication to this Path,

And bless my efforts.

Light the Spirit candle, and blow out the one that represents the old life. Say,

> Today is a new beginning.
>
> And here before the Watchtowers,
>
> Ancient ones, and you,
>
> I declare my intention to practice Cyber Magick
>
> And walk the Path of Beauty.

Self Blessing

Pick up the bottle of oil and dab it where noted reciting its affirmation:

Forehead:

> Bless my mind for refreshed perspective and ingenuity.

Eyes:

> Bless my eyes to see magickal potential in all things.

Lips:

> Bless my lips to speak the truth in love.

Heart:

> Bless my heart to freely give and receive.

Feet:

> Bless my feet that they may never stray from the path of greatest good.

Light the second candle that represents your new Path, and say,

> Goddess and God above and below me,
>
> Goddess and God behind and before me.
>
> Magick within and without.
>
> So mote it be!

Now, take some time to write in your journal about your hopes and wishes for the future, and how you see Cyber Magic transforming your reality. When you're done writing, recite those wishes into the bowl of petals, then release them out the window to be carried to all of creation.

Closing the Ritual

First, say a prayer from your heart (aloud or silently). It needs to come from your soul. Just say what's on your mind, deep down in your soul, right at this moment and take a moment to listen to Spirit's voice speaking back. After a few minutes of introspection, dismiss the Quarters by saying,

> Earth and Air, Fire, and Sea
>
> Thank you for coming and blessing me.
>
> Air and Earth, Water, and Fire
>
> Thank you for granting my heart's desire.
>
> Hail and Farewell. Blessed be!

After the Ritual

Eat something. This will help to ground you and bring you back to a normal state of awareness. Next, share your experience with another magickal friend (or in keeping with

Cyber Witchery, e-mail him or her!). Finally, take some time studying your Craft online or pick up a good book and read. Today is an important day and it should celebrate who you are and who you hope to become as a magickal Being.

Just for Fun

In our intense field studies of the customs, characteristics, and habits of the Cyber Witch in her or his favorite habitat, we've discovered some interesting similitude. Compare yourself to this tell-tale list, for you too might be a Cyber Witch if:

✳ Windows2000 to the Gods is installed on your operating system.

✳ You divine by Iconology.

✳ Your broom (unlike your computer) never crashes.

✳ You use the recycle bin on your computer as a banishing spell.

✳ When a spell or ritual isn't working right, you reboot it.

✳ You've found candle wax on your cell phone.

✳ Your totem animal is a mouse.

✳ McAffee is part of your regular warding process.

✳ You bless your computer regularly with a defrag ritual.

✳ Your mouse pads have pentagrams or other sigils that can be traced to evoke the magick.

✳ Your chalice is a non-spillable sports bottle or travel mug.

✳ Your three-finger lunar salute is Ctl, Alt, Del.

✳ You have "nuked" your spell components.

✳ Casting a spell includes pushing a "send" key.

✳ You check to see if the surge protector is turned on before casting a spell.

✳ You use a computer or TV screen as a scrying-surface.

✳ Your domain name is your Circle name.

✳ You check *www.witchvox.com* more than once a week for information.

✳ Your Book of Shadows is burned on a CD (complete with online manual).

✳ Your favorite coven is a chat room.

✳ Your curses have real byte.

✳ Cakes are fine, but only virtual wine is allowed near keyboards.

✳ If it's broken your first thought is either reboot, reformat, unplug and plug back in, or "get the duct tape."

✳ You have gods with names such as Bit and Rom.

✳ The Threefold Law says: Everything shall be backed up in three places.

✳ Your Rede says: Do as you will, but spam none.

With the basics out of the way, and having taken the first step down the Path of Cyber Witchery, let's move on now to study the intricacies of creating and maintaining sacred space, and the role of gods and goddesses in this unique tradition. Although you've already had a brief taste of sacred space and the presence of Spirit in your dedication, we'd like to take the time and put the whole process into perspective.

As you read on, please remember to take your time. There's no need to hurry. Just because technology moves fast doesn't mean that the spiritual application of it has to come quickly. No one becomes and adept Cyber Witch overnight. However, we can promise that curiosity, consistency, and cleverness will eventually pay off for you, even as it has for us two very dedicated Cyber Witches, who even went so far as to write this whole book without paper!

Sacred Space and Cyber Magick Deities

Before launching into this part of the book, it's important to remember that most people, but not all, use Goddesses and Gods in spellcrafting and ritual. Why? Quite simply because for some individuals magick is more a way of doing things (a philosophy) as opposed to a spiritual conviction.

We both do work in rapport with Goddesses and Gods. Divine energy is what really powers all successful magick! When it comes to the importance of sacred space and Deity, we feel that even those readers who prefer not to work with a Goddess or God can utilize the concept of sacred space successfully. It's important for everyone to understand the symbolic value of Deity in Cyber Craft.

Sacred Space

What is sacred? It's an honest question deserving of an honest answer. At one time in history what was holy was totally delineated by the ruling authority (king, chieftain, or priest). Today, however, things are different.

Wicca and many other Neo-Pagan traditions advocate being your own priestess or priest. We choose our sacred Path and we make our own decisions regarding our faith. As incarnations of the Divine, we are not separate from Deity. We are one with Deity—all faces of the Divine.

In other words, we are taking moral and ethical responsibility for our actions or inactions both substantively and magickally. As a diverse group of people with faith in the sacred land, the Goddess, and God, we have the power in our hearts and hands to create positive changes in the world right now and in the future. This can be both an empowering and uncomfortable concept, and one that requires a little adjustment.

What's important to remember here is that each of us already acts in this capacity to some degree. Whenever we make a choice, whenever we give thoughtful advice to a friend, whenever we show compassion, we are acting in the capacity of a spiritual helpmate. We reveal our divine nature. Because Cyber Witches, as do other Witches, view life itself as the altar, each of these actions can have sacred energies associated with them. In fact, every moment, thought, action, feeling, and breath, is sacred! You just have to reach that awareness. The main difference is your outlook and attitude.

Just as we hope that you wouldn't go skipping through a church with muddy shoes because that space is holy to a group of people, that's exactly how sacredness works in a Cyber Witch's home, Circle, office, and daily routine. By approaching each moment as an opportunity to express magick and ideals, we make that moment special. We make it divine. Cyber Witches are true spiritual opportunists. By remaining attentive, present, and aware of that opportunity, we can also make the most of it!

That said, there are certainly times in which even the "Kitchen Witch" or "Techno-Pagan" practitioner will want a more formalized sense of sacredness and protection. Whether it is for an important spell, ritual, meditation, or gathering, there are certainly occasions that inspire us to seek out the helpful powers, commune with them, and raise magick within the sphere of their watchful eye.

The question then becomes one of how the Cyber Witch designates and creates sacred space. True to form, the answer to this question is highly personalized and creative. We would like to offer you some ideas to play with and adapt to your own space and vision.

Informal Sacred Space

First, let's consider less formalized sacred space. There are many circumstances in life that don't allow for a full, formal Circle. At the office, at a hotel convention, or in front of the Catholic in-laws, probably aren't the best circumstances in which to don a robe, wield a wand, and chant an invocation to the Goddess!

As Cyber Witches, we realize our world is not wholly Pagan and we avoid imposing our beliefs on others by our practices. So what do you do when you want to raise sacred energies in these types of situations? Trish's approach is to literally take the sacred space on the road. To accomplish this, begin by choosing small, inexpensive, portable items, and charge them with Elemental energy. If you're unfamiliar with the idea of charging, it basically means filling each item with the vibrations desired.

You have thousands of choices for components. Try four different colored crystals, beans, toothpicks, tiddlywinks, poker chips, flower petals, or paper clips. Whenever possible, however, we do recommend coordinating the chosen items so that they symbolize the Element. For example, a green toothpick is good for Earth, as is a plain one because it's made from wood. Meanwhile, flower petals can be chosen by the Elemental correspondences all of Nature bears.

Once you've figured out what you want to use, the chosen items should be exposed to the proper Watchtower's energy. For example, the next time you cast a Circle at home, put a white pebble in the East in front of a fan, a red one in the South near a burning candle or brazier, a blue one in the West in a cup of water, and a green or brown one in the North in some rich soil. Let these simply absorb the sacred energies you've created and the power of the nearby Element. Sometime before you are finished with your spell, tell each stone its activating word (*Now* is a good one). Deconstruct your Circle and take the stones with you so they're available for later use.

Carry the charged items in a power pouch until they're needed. At that point, take them out and place each as close as possible to the directional point it is connected with. As the items take their spots, whisper (or think) the activating word to them. Moving slowly, with intention, the Circle goes in place without anyone being unnerved by it. When you do this quietly, no one even notices, except for the other Witches, of course.

When you're done with whatever magick you were working, it's up to you to decide if you want to regather the components or not. If you like, you can leave them in place. They'll simply radiate blessing to that spot, the energy slowly dissipating like it might from a battery. On the other hand, if you do gather them, you can refill and use them again. The only precaution here is to make sure you use that set for the same magickal purpose in the future. Consistency and continuity is important to manifestation.

Another easy way to take the sacred space "on the road" is by making portable altars for your car, purse, suitcase, or briefcase. This can be done using a solidly constructed pouch or one of those craft balls that can be opened and filled. Remember to avoid anything breakable. If our ancestors had plastic, you can bet they would have used it! At the same time, keep in mind that metals, stones, woods, and natural objects take and hold a more powerful magickal field charge than plastic items. They still hold a charge—most anything will—but it means you will need to charge plastic items more frequently.

Take the pouch, craft ball, or other properly sized container and fill it with ashes from a sacred Fire, a match (to represent the burning of that fire), a crystal or acorn for Earth, a seashell for Water, and a feather for Air. Note that these are just suggestions. Use your own creative juices and intuition to decide what you want in your portable altar. When everything is in place, empower the item by saying,

> Earth and Air, Fire and foam,
>
> No matter where I roam,
>
> Bring me safely back to home.
>
> Fire and Water, Earth and Air, The power of the Elements, With me, bear.
>
> Air and Fire, Earth and sea,
>
> By my will,
>
> So mote it be!

Now tuck that item safely in something you carry regularly. Trish hangs hers on the rear view mirror of her car.

This way the movements of the car put the magick in motion! Sirona keeps her portable pouch in her purse, activating it when she carries her purse.

Now we've covered being outside the house, but what about times when you feel you can't create a formal Circle within your home? Perhaps time is lacking, or perhaps your non-Pagan roommates just wouldn't understand. When this happens, firstly, remember that *you* are your own sacred space. Your body is the temple of spirit and your mind its conduit—that makes you holy. Because most of us forget that we are divine, that we are Goddess and God, we just have to learn how to activate that power.

Secondly, remember that our minds, as the conduit of spirit, are pretty amazing things. You can hold an entire ritual in the mundania of your mental space, if you wish. Within the sacred space of self (or any sacred space) everything becomes as powerful as that which it represents, even visualizations! There's nothing keeping the Cyber Witch from invoking and reveling in sacred space any time, anywhere, so long as she or he can maintain focus. Go ahead and light a candle, dab on a favorite scented oil, and put on some music. Most of us truly enjoy these sensual additions and they serve to support the overall internal ambiance you're creating.

Third, keep in mind that the ideas presented for outside the home also work within that space. It's pretty easy to decoratively place some crystals, coins, and statues, on bookshelves, TV stands, and coffee tables, without evoking odd looks. Although hanging out in the kitchen may feel a little different after all your appliances have been magickally blessed and charged, only you know that you have consecrated your techno-tools. It's only you who need to understand the significance, and as with the previous examples, these items can remain spiritually neutral until you call them into action.

Fourth, home altars need not be anything that someone else would object to. Trish's two favorite altars are a bookshelf and a computer desk, neither one of which screams *Witch* by its appearance (unless you read the book titles!). On the computer desk, for example, there's a goblet filled with pens, pencils, rubber bands, and scissors. This neatly represents the Water element and serves a valuable mundane function too! Her Rolodex is black (for Earth), the desk lamp becomes Fire, and the Sylph painting above the desk is Air. In this way, all the powers of the sacred space surround no matter what may be happening in the home. You can do something similar.

What we're trying to stress through all these examples is that any situation, circumstance, and moment in the day can be (and often is) the right time for magick. You might just have to be a little inventive and figure out how that magick plays itself out. Cyber Witches love that kind of challenge because it gives us a chance, once again, to examine everything in this world for it's spiritual potential, then put that potential to work for us.

Formal Sacred Space

With the informal sacred space issues handled, what about those times when the Cyber Witch craves something more formal? Just because our technological society has fattened us with fast food, doesn't mean that it satisfies, and such is also the case with "quick-spell" kinds of magick. Instant sacred space doesn't always cut it, especially for important or pressing matters.

Cyber Witches recognize the real value in taking the time to build energy from the ground up within a protected sphere. Just like putting one's finger in the dam, the formal sacred space protects us from the flood of energy from the outside world, and keeps the waters of magick firmly in place until we're ready to release and guide that energy. But what exactly constitutes sacred space for a Cyber Witch?

The differences here are really more in form and tools than in the intention, construction, and effects. After all, sacred space still marks the line between the worlds. It continues to create a safe haven for those within it, and certainly manifests a distinctly different energy than a less formal magickal working. In casting the Circle, the Cyber Witch uses visualization, incantations, movement, and symbolism, just as those Witches working with other systems.

All Witches understand the importance of staying in tune with the current ways of our times. What we need to look at are the representative elements we bring into the space in which we're working, and also in some cases, the crafting of our spells. Looking first at our Quarter points, now rather than candles, incense, chalices, and crystals, we use a battery operated lamp (which is also fire safe), potpourri, a coffee mug, and a globe! When you plan it right, you can arrange items already present in your sacred space accordingly. A great deal of the time they might work perfectly well just where they sit. For example, Trish's hot tub happens to be in the West of her home, so she just turns it on when she's doing the western invocation to let that energy flow! Similarly, she has a lizard terrarium in the South, so she turns on the red nightlights to accent that Fire energy.

Similar adaptations can take place on the altar too. If it's readily available and bears all the appropriate symbolic value, the Cyber Witch's code is *use it*! The only precaution is to properly cleanse, charge, and bless all such items so they don't carry any unwanted energy into your sacred space. Cleansing can be accomplished simply with sage smoke or a little lemon or salt water. Charging by sunlight or moonlight is certainly apt, and you can use whatever forms of blessing you feel comfortable with. Cybcr Witchcs tcnd to bc innova-tive, and that's a spirit that we strongly advocate!

Calling in the Cyber Quarters

In terms of wording, we suggest that you dispense with Old English and Shakespearian prose. It doesn't exactly roll smoothly off most Cyber Witches' tongues—and a lot of people just plain don't understand what the heck you are saying! Use modern words and phrases. You will find that those participating, including yourself, will relate to them much better. When you adapt or write your invocations think about words you use every day as potential substitutes for words that have an antiquated feel. For example, "thou" becomes "you" and "hail" becomes "greetings." You can even call on the Goddess saying, "Yo, Mama, come on down!" As long as it's a respectful plea and all in good fun, it works rather nicely. Techno-Pagans know that magick can be the leading edge, exciting, fun, simple, and quickly done. The key is maintaining your respectfulness and intention.

The following is an example of an updated Cyber Witch Quarter calling. You can use it as is or tweak it to better suit your style and needs.

Face East and say,

Greetings, Protectors of the East. Be welcome here. Fill this space with your vital breath and hold this Circle in safety. (This might be a perfect time to turn on an electric fan.)

Face South and say,

Greetings, Protectors of the South. Be welcome here. Fill this space with your warmth and energy and hold this Circle in safety. (Turn on a lamp or heater).

Face West and say,

Greetings, Protectors of the West. Be welcome here. Fill this space with your healing waters and hold this Circle in safety. (Turn on a water faucet, hot tub, washing machine, dishwasher, or a tabletop fountain.)

Face North and say,

Greetings, Protectors of the North. Be welcome here. Fill this space with your strong foundations and hold this Circle in safety. (Turn on your breadmaker, connect to magnets, activate a talking toy animal, or plant a seed in a cup of dirt.)

Stand in the Center of your Circle, and say,

Greetings, Great Spirit. Be welcome here. Watch over the magick I create today, and guide it for the greatest good, while you hold this Circle in safety. Note: What you do when invoking spirit may change depending on the God or Goddess you work with, but we suggest that you still light a candle on this one. The symbolism just plain works and it sets the tone for making magick.

The Body of the Cyber Spell

Once the sacred space is erected, what happens within it is up to you. However, there are some good hints to enacting effective spells that we'd like to share briefly with those newer to magick. First, rituals need a defined beginning, body, and end. Calling the Watchtowers or Quarters is a very good beginning as it directs our minds away from mundania.

The body of the ritual can take a lot of forms, depending on your goal. Some people will work spells, some may weave sacred dances, and others still will meditate or pray to raise energy. Whatever your process, it needs to make sense and maintain a symbolic continuity in terms of the type of energy you're trying to gather. For example, if you're crafting a spell to halt gossip, a lot of noise doesn't make sense. When you're trying to quiet things down, work in total silence and include a binding spell.

Many rituals close rather naturally with the release of the energy created. Other endings might include a closing prayer, snuffing out candles, or deconstructing the Circle. Additionally, we recommend some type of grounding activity at this juncture or right after the close of the Circle. One idea is simply having after-magick snacks as sort of a mini-feast. Hey, what a great reason to enjoy some good food!

Another characteristic of a successful ritual is that it has been carefully thought out and enacted. Throughout the ritual, maintaining one's focus and remaining open to Spirit's leadings is vital. Additionally, pay attention to your own leadings and instincts.

Bear in mind that sometimes our energy doesn't manifest exactly as we plan. This is true in spells, too. Even the most forward-thinking, proactive Cyber Witch is bound to mess up from time to time or find out the Universe has other plans. Be open to both experiences. The first will teach you much about yourself and your art and Craft. The second teaches you about Universal Laws and patterns. Both learning experiences are worthwhile as they serve to expand your awareness and magickal ability.

Your Cyber Book of Shadows

More Techno-Pagan than traditional, your Cyber Book of Shadows is a computerized journal. It's a Witch's diary of spells, potions, and rituals, as well as thoughts, impressions, ideas, pictures, paintings, and notes. It's always a good idea to make notes of your spellcrafting, shortly after you do it. Write the results, noting what worked and what didn't. You can refer back to your notes in the future to know which symbols, pictures, music, techno-tools, Web sites, and words were more powerful, and which ones fell flat.

Your Cyber Book of Shadows can be stored on your hard drive and/or floppy disk. We suggest you back it up. Bless and charge your Cyber Book of Shadows directory or file by saying,

> I call you Great Cyber Ones, Divine Ones
>
> Bless this Cyber Book each passing hour.
>
> By space, Earth, Fire, and sea
>
> Charge it with your sacred power.
>
> As I will, so shall it be!

Feel free to tweak the blessing and charge to better suit your style, language, and needs.

You can add a simple chant before you save files in your Cyber Book of Shadows directory by saying something such as,

> Save this power
>
> May it flower
>
> Blessed be!

A lot of Pagan Internet sites offer practical information, spells, rituals, and graphics. For example, you can go to any search engine and type in "love spells" or "Pagan spells." Click on the ones you like, and then download them into your Cyber Book of Shadows. You can add Cyber Magick spells you collect along the way from friends, books such as this one, and magazines.

Chat transcripts can also be saved in your Cyber Book of Shadows. When you do a chat, ask where it will be posted and make a note of the Web address. Go to the site and download the chat, create a file, and name it. Or cut and paste part of a chat, and put it in a file and name it, for example if you chatted on May Day, call it "Beltane Chat."

For visual power, add pictures, animated GIFs, photographs, favorite paintings, and sound. All of these can be loaded, scanned, or copied from the Internet or CDs for your personal, but *not* commercial, use.

Before you die, it is customary to pass your Book of Shadows, and this includes your Cyber Book of Shadows, on to your children or a trusted friend. This keeps the knowledge and magick alive!

Downloading Deity

As we mentioned at the beginning of this chapter, most Pagans, Wiccans, or Witches, like ourselves, work with Deity. But to which Goddesses and Gods does the Cyber Witch turn? That's a good question, one that needs a bit of creative elbow room to ponder.

There are certainly thousands of Goddesses and Gods from around the world whose imagery evokes positive responses, but because our ancestors didn't have the kinds of technology we do, it's time to tweak the aspects of the Goddesses and Gods just a bit. For example, because the Celtic Goddess Epona's sacred animal was a horse, she is a suitable Goddess to call upon for protecting our automobiles (the horse being an earlier form of transportation). Similarly, Spider Woman and the Fates become networking powers, whose lines stretch out and help keep us connected.

For Cyber Witches, technology offers some interesting magickal twists. For example, during a Drawing Down of the Moon, you can download graphics and information on a specific Goddess from the Internet so that the image of the Goddess fills the computer even as she fills your sacred space and heart! Alternatively, have an image of that Goddess on your palm pilot (this is especially handy when you're on the road).

Techno-Pagans often joke about newly emerging Goddesses and Gods such as the great Caffeina and Squat. Caffeina, of course, presides over our coffee and teapots, and Squat is the God of good parking spaces (we understand he accepts quarters as offerings). This sounds a little silly, but given some serious thought, there's no reason why we cannot create new mythologies based on the world as it is today, and the techno-tools in it. That's what our ancestors did when they envisioned the sacred in a fashion suited to their culture and era.

Over time, "thought forms" begin to have viable power as long as that form receives proper honors in your life. Thought equals energy. So if you choose to venerate Snap (the God of microwaved foods), Click (the computer mouse Goddess), Popup (the Goddess of toasters and toaster ovens), Ram and Rom (the computer twin Gods), Bit and Byte (the computer twin Goddesses), or Wireless (the spirit of cell phones), go for it! Just remember that such interactions won't be quite the same as traditional deities because they're younger and still gaining power.

The following list of deities can be called upon when doing cyber spells and making magick. Work with several of the Goddesses and Gods to discover your favorites.

Cyber Magick Deities

Abnoba:
A Celtic Goddess of the hunt, she would be ideal for online shopping sprees, hunting for old classmates, and looking for like-minded people on the Internet.

Adonis:
He is a Greek God of beauty and love who is helpful when you looking to invoke a God to power your cyber love spells.

Aegir:
A Scandinavian sea God on whom you would call for protection before going on a cruise. He is best appeased with a gift of some sort.

Aengus mac Og (Angus, Angus Og, Oengus):
A Celtic God of love and beauty. Aengus is the ideal e-mail and cyber romance deity. He is the healer of souls and helps with romance and courting.

Aeolus:
A three-headed Greek God of the winds with four arms (North, East, South, and West). His home is a floating island called Lipali. Call upon him when working with techno-tools such as fans or items with fans such as computer printers, air conditioners, heaters, and the like. He is also a great special effects and computer graphics deity.

Agni:
As the Hindu Fire God born in wood, he is a cyber Fire God of heaters, furnaces, fireplaces, and woodstoves. Invite him in when turning on lamps, your flashlight, virtual balefires on your computer screen, or when you flip on the heater thermostat.

Ailinn: Celtic Goddess of affection, love, and cyber romance.

Aine: Celtic Earth and solar Goddess of the Summer Solstice and Midsummer's Eve with Finn as her consort. Sorceress and Queen of the Faery, begotten by the spirits of Fire and night, she can help you rid your computer of pixies. The one to call upon when doing Cyber Faery Magick or installing a solar system.

Airmed: As the Celtic Goddess of Witchcraft, she can make your cyber spells much more powerful.

Aker: As an Egyptian God who sees in both directions, this is a good entity to look to when East meets West in your practices or when you are seeking any type of balance.

Akupera: Hindu Cyber Goddess of moonlight you can call upon when doing your cyber spells at night during the light of the moon.

Ala: Nigerian Earth Mother Goddess of fertility and plenty. Call upon before using your charge cards.

Alom: A Mayan Mother Goddess who can be invoked in fertility magick when you want to carry a boy. Scan photos and pick graphics from the Internet to fill your computer screen with pictures of adorable boys, especially boys you know personally, and then chant Alom's name several times to bring that boy child energy into your home over the cyber waves.

Amaethon:	A Celtic God of the garden, who is called the "Harvest King." Associated with the fruits of the harvest, as well as the sickle, hoe, plow, garden and lawn tractor, and rototiller, you can call on him when you are working with your techno-tools outdoors. Also call on him any time you need to clear the way for your energy or when reconfiguring your computer system.
Amon:	He is an Egyptian primal creation God, who is also the Cyber God of cloning.
Anadyomene:	Greek sea-born Goddess of sexuality; call upon her when doing Cyber Love Magick.
Anahita:	Persian "Golden Mother," who is healer, mother, and protector. Use her to protect your computer, particularly from viruses, hackers, and the like.
Anna Perenna:	She is a Roman Goddess of cyber sexuality and fertility.
Annapurna:	Hindu Great Mother Goddess of abundance and giver of plenty, she can make your Web site profitable, within the cyber world.
Ansar:	The Babylonian "host of heaven"; call upon this being when traveling by Air, or to bless your telescope.
Anuket, Anukis:	Egyptian Goddess of rivers and fertility. In the modern sense, the river is the Internet and fertility reflects the rewards you reap from it.
Aobh:	A Celtic Goddess who controls the flow of the Internet; invoke her when you want a faster computer connection.

Aphrodite: The ultimate Greek Goddess of love, pleasure, and beauty; invoke her when you mean business when doing cyber love spells.

Apollo: Greek God of solar power, poetry, creative arts, music, healing, and divination. For creative ventures, Apollo helps bring in the creative energies that are essential for success. Call on Apollo to bless your e-mail system, telephone, fax machine, solar panels, or cell phone.

Arawn: Celtic God of death, war, and ancestry and the King of Annwn, the Underworld. Invoke his powers when you want to shapeshift a cyber situation, such as when something doesn't work and you want to change it into something that does work for you.

Ariadne: Greek Goddess of labyrinths and virus detection software who can unravel cyber mysteries.

Arianrhod: She is a powerful Celtic Stellar and Lunar Goddess, who is the keeper of the "Silver Wheel" or "Silver Disc." Call upon her when doing Cyber Moon Magick and wishing upon a virtual star.

Artemis: Greek Goddess of cyber abundance and twin sister of Apollo, she is helpful for having a fruitful and complementary relationship with the machines in your life.

Artio: As a Celtic Goddess of fertility portrayed as a bear, she is the Goddess of energy that powers all cyber functions from your toaster popping up to clocks telling the right time.

Astarte:	She is the Assyro-Babylonian Great Mother Goddess, associated with the planet Venus. Akin to a motherboard that runs computer networks, she is the command center that makes all your cyber connections run together as a whole. Call her in when you are doing Cyber Magick in the morning.
Athena:	She is the Greek Goddess of wisdom and warriors in battle. In cyber terms, this means that in one sense, humans see themselves at war with machines, but in another sense they know machines are tools for making life better— that is, as long as humans control the machines and not the other way around. Invoke Athena when you want to make your life better by using mechanical and electronic devices more wisely.
Atum:	An Egyptian deity who is both female and male, she is complete, whole, and perfect. Mass without form, she is both everything and nothing at the same time. Representing a cyber deity of oneness, she makes the machines in your life run at their optimum.
Baduh:	This Semitic God of speedy messages is ideal for the Internet and e-mail.
Banba:	She is the Celtic Earth Goddess who represents the sacred machine, where all parts work both independently and together as a whole.
Bannik:	He is the Slavonic God of the wash house who is ideal for blessing the hot tub or sauna (not to mention your shower and bathtub).

Bast, Bastet: Egyptian Cat Goddess of fertility, pleasure, dancing, music, and love. She is protectress of your home and car music systems.

Bel, Bile, Belenos: Celtic God of solar power, light, and healing, referred to as "The Shining One." He is associated with the source of all light, including all the lights in your house.

Belisama: She is a young Celtic Fire Goddess associated with the rising sun whose name means "like unto flame" and "the bright and shining one." The power switches in Cyber Magick techno-tools are under her domain as are solar-powered techno-tools.

Bhaga: He is a Hindu God who brings marriage, fortune, and prosperity to your cyber altar.

Blathnat: "Little Flower," Celtic Goddess of sex, Blathnat helps in the joining of Cyber Magick components and tools, for example computers and printers, CDs and CD players, videos and video players, and so forth.

Boann, Boi, Boanna:
The Celtic Mother of the herds, she is the source of cyber inspiration and the reason all your electrical devices work so well together. Call her in when paying your Internet bill or purchasing a computer system.

Bochica: He is a Columbian God who gave people the first calendar system, so let him preside over your date book or organizer!

Borvo, Bormo, Bormanus:

He is the Celtic Golden God of healing, the unseen and concealed truth, and inspiration gained through dreams. Also associated with hot springs and hot tubs.

Bragi:

Call this Norse God of poetry in to help you get your poetry posted up on the Internet and published.

Bran or Bron:

He is a Celtic God of music and prophecy, protector of bards and poets, and associated with singing, the bard's harp, and the Sacred Head. In the modern sense, he is the God of electronic keyboards, synthesizers, and MIDI.

Branwen:

This Celtic Goddess of love, called the "White-Bosomed One" and "Venus of the Northern Sea," can be invited into your cyber space when doing Love Magick.

Bridget, Brighid, Brede, Bride:

She is the Celtic fertility Goddess of the sacred Fire. She is the bride and the Goddess of inspiration, love, poetry, medicine, healing, and smithcraft. It is she who protects all musical and surgical instruments, as well as electronic devices such as stereos, TVs, and computers.

Brigantia:

Associated with the rivers, mountains, and valleys of the countryside, she is the Goddess of Nature and solar energy. In her modern guise she inhabits tabletop fountains, indoor waterfalls, indoor water spheres, solar panels, and virtual retreats.

Buddha:　The name "Buddha" means enlightened one, so you can invoke him to empower all light sources, or anything you turn on, which also symbolizes our spiritual awakenings. A God of solar energy and zero point energy, he embodies the wisdom of solar power and "free" energy in calculators, radios, toys, laptops, homes, and automobiles. Buddha is a mindful and peaceful cyber deity who gives as you give, thinks as you think, exists as you exist.

Cailleach:　She is a pre-Celtic Goddess of the Earth, sky, moon, and sun who controlled the seasons and weather. Call her in when you are calling up the weather on the Internet.

Calliope:　The Greek Muse of epic poetry is an excellent cyber helpmate, especially when you are trying to find the best wording for a spell or ritual.

Cesara:　A Celtic Mother Goddess who, in Irish stories, led an expedition 40 days before the great flood. Call on her to inspire adventure, to bless travel, or to support the human quest to reach skyward.

Chandra:　A Hindu God who was born of the churning ocean. A potential pantry protector especially for things such as food processors and blenders.

Chango:　African love God, drummer, dancer, and king who can be asked to preside over Cyber Love Magick.

Chokmah:	In the Tree of Life, this is raw energy. Call on this God to watch over all power sources, on-off switches, surge protectors, plugs, and wires.
Clio:	The Greek Muse of history. Call her in when surfing archives or collecting information on the Internet.
Cliodna:	"Shapely One," Celtic Bird Goddess and Faery Queen, she is an extraordinary fair-haired beauty, known for her abilities at shapeshifting. She might do well presiding over beauticians and salons.
Condatis:	He is a Celtic Cyber Water God of fountains, washing machines, dishwashers, sinks, bathtubs, and faucets.
Cordemanon:	A Celtic God of travel, trains, buses, airplanes, boats, ships, hovercraft, helicopters, and subways, he is also a God of knowledge and ancestry, associated with stone circles and sacred sites.
Coventina:	A Celtic Goddess of the well and the womb of the Earth, she presides over tabletop fountains, swimming pools, bathtubs, hot springs, and hot tubs. She is associated with healing springs, sacred wells, childbirth, renewal, and the Earth.

Creidne or Creidhne, Credne:

The Celtic Master Sword Maker named "The Bronze Worker." Associated with smiths, wrights, metal-working, and craftspersons, ask him to bless all machine-made items.

Cronus: As the Greek and Phoenician guardian of time, call on him to preside over timers, watches, and clocks.

Cu Chulainn: In Celtic mythology he is the Hound of Culain, born with the strength of a man and a burning rage to conquer all in his path. Virtual and robotic dogs are his Cyber Magick power animals.

Cupid: Here is a Roman God of love you can call upon when playing darts, doing cyber love spells, and sending romantic e-cards.

Dagda: He is the Celtic "Good God" and "Good Hand." Chieftain Earth God of life, death, wisdom, prosperity, pleasure, and feasting. As a God of knowledge, invite him in when you are on the Internet, before watching a video, or before business calls. His tools are oak trees, a magickal sword, the club, an inexhaustible cauldron, a magickal harp, the chalice, and the rods of command.

Daikoku: The Japanese God of luck and wealth; give him dominion over your checkbook, credit cards, the stock market, and checking account.

Dana, Danu, Anu: The Celtic Mother Goddess from whom Tuatha De Danann were descended, she is a shapeshifter and Goddess of wisdom and creation. She is an excellent helpmate when doing any kind of Cyber Magick.

Deirdre: "One who gives warning," or the older form Derdriu, "Oak prophet," she is the Goddess of virus protection software.

Demeter: A Greek Goddess of fertility, marriage, and prosperity who can help you with your cyber love spells.

Deus Fidius: A Roman God of hospitality, call on him for favor when traveling.

Devi: A Hindu Goddess whose energy continues to protect the world from chaos, she stops all machines from breaking down all at once.

Diana: The Roman Goddess of moonlight and the hunt; you can call upon when doing Cyber Moon Magick.

Dianacht: Look to this Celtic "God of Curing" or "Swift in Power" for help in finding the right family physician, specialist, acupuncturist, herbalist, or holistic professional. Healing physician to the Gods, he is associated with the mortar and pestle and thus the ideal coffee grinder God to call upon when making your potions.

Dionysus: From pastoral beginnings, associated with goat herding, he became the Greek God of ecstasy, sex, revelry, and pleasure. Call upon him when doing cyber love spells.

Du: He is an Egyptian God who can be invoked when you need to live more presently and attentively.

Dumiatis, Dumeatis:
Celtic God of creative thought and teaching, audio books, educational CDs, and cable stations such as PBS and Discovery are all under his domain. Call upon him when you are making film documentaries or home videos.

Dwyane: A Celtic God of love and mischief, invite him in when viewing joke-a-day type sites on the Internet.

Edain, Etain: Celtic Goddess of beauty, grace, and wife of King Mider, she is one of the "White Ladies" of the Faery and can be called in when doing Cyber Faery Magick.

El: The Semitic "Old King," El is an exceptionally good God on which to call for blessing our elders, especially now that a great deal of the world's population is living much longer.

Eostre or Ostara: She is the Celtic Goddess of candy, eggs, Spring, and fertility.

Epona: She is a Celtic horse Goddess, whose strength and protective power can be called upon when you are riding on a merry-go-round, when you are driving in your car or traveling on trains or buses, and when you are riding horses. She is also a Goddess of fertility, power, and abundance.

Erato: The Greek muse of love poetry, mimicry, and pantomime; cameras of all kinds are this deity's domain, as are holographs and tape recorders.

Erie, Eriu: She is the triple Celtic Mother Goddess of Erin, sometimes known as Ir, from which Ireland, the land of Ir, is derived. Shapeshifter and Goddess of Sovereignty of the Land, call upon her when you are looking at real estate on the Internet.

Eros:
: As a Greek God of passionate love, he is the "R" rated and "X" rated God of sexuality.

Esus:
: A Celtic woodland God associated with hunting, the sword, the Golden Bull, and the bow and arrow, he is the ancient woodcutter. The chainsaw is his modern-day ritual tool.

Eurynome:
: She is the Greek Mother of all pleasure, whose embodiment is the beautiful triplets, the Graces: splendor, abundance, and joyousness. Call her in when you want to put a little style into your Cyber Magick.

Euterpe:
: As the Greek muse of music and lyric poetry, you can call upon her to protect your CDs, CD player, radio, stereo, and other musical related techno-tools.

Evander:
: He is the Roman God credited with adapting Greek letters into the Roman alphabet. This God might be suited for our various translation needs both in human and computer languages.

Ezili:
: This Haitian Goddess is generous to the point of extravagance with her followers and expects the same in return. She is the ideal Goddess of credit cards.

Fal:
: This Celtic God has a wheel of light, with which he can perform great magick, including flying through the air. He is a God of airplanes, helicopters, and spaceships.

Fand: Celtic shapeshifter and Faery Queen of Ireland, she is the seagull Goddess who protects you on ocean voyages, on boats, and when you are vacationing at enchanting retreats and getaways. Daughter of the sea, she is the ruler of the magickal "Land Over Wave," a Celtic paradise.

Faunus: An ancient Roman Nature God who can help us keep in touch with the Earth and her energies even in the concrete jungle.

Fengi and Mengi: Two Norse magickal giants, who in the time of the heroic Scandinavian King Frodi, worked a mill whose grindstone magickally produced peace and prosperity. Call upon them to strengthen your prosperity spells.

Findabair: She is the Celtic Goddess of Connacht and the Otherworld, of beauty, grace, and love. Techno-tools for beautification such as hair dryers, electric shavers, curling irons, electric curlers are under her domain, as are make-up professionals and cosmetic companies.

Fliodhas: Celtic Goddess of the woodlands and protector of animals and forests, she is associated with the doe.

Flora: She is the Roman Goddess of fertility, sex, promiscuity, and Spring. Call upon her when you are doing pregnancy testing, before making love, and to bless safe sex items such as condoms.

Fortuna: A Roman Goddess of love and sexuality, called Lady Luck; round things of fortune such as roulette wheels are under her domain.

Frey: He is the Norse God of fertility, joy, peace, and happiness.

Freya: She is the Norse Goddess of love, beauty, passion, and fertility.

Frigga: The Norse Goddess of feminine arts, associated with hawks and falcons, call upon her to bless and protect you when traveling by Air.

Gaea: The Greek Mother Goddess who embodies the Earth and has existed since before time began, she is an excellent deity to call upon for all kinds of Cyber Magick and ritual. Also invoke her when working with alternate energy sources such as solar, wind, and zero point energy.

Ganesa: A Hindu God of luck, wisdom, and writings, he is an excellent patron for emerging New Age writers and speakers.

Geburah: Cabalistic destroyer of those things that are worn-out or negative; let him preside over your recycling bins and compost.

Gobannon or Govannon, Goibniu:
    The Divine Smith and Celtic God of magick, also called "Gobban the Wright" and "Gobban Saer, The Master Mason," he is the God of all metals and smelting ovens. He can be called upon when using techno-tools with blades, for example, can openers, food processors, and circular saws.

Graces [Roman, Greeks called them the Charities]:

These three Goddesses embody grace of manner. They are Thaleia (abundance), Aglaia (splendor and radiance), and Eurphrosyne (joy and happiness).

Grainne:

A young Celtic sun maiden who becomes a Goddess of love, she is an ideal Goddess to call upon when installing your solar system or entering a tanning salon.

Gwalchmei:

Celtic God of love and music and son of the Goddess, Mei, he is called the "Hawk of May." Call to him and ask him for his blessing and power when you see a hawk while driving in your car.

Gwydion:

A Celtic shapeshifter and Celtic God of the arts, he is the ideal God to call upon when doing special effects on your computer. A God of eloquence, humanity, and kindness, ask him to help you in chat rooms and when you send e-mail.

Harmonia:

Greek Goddess of music, especially rock 'n' roll, dance, and poetry, you can call upon her to bless and protect your stereo, radio, computer, VCR, digital recorder, and electronic equipment such as electric guitars, keyboards, and amplifiers.

Hathor:

She is an Egyptian Goddess of love, Mother of creation, and mistress of everything that is beautiful.

Heimdall:	A Norse God who guards the rainbow bridge and is known for his incredible sight and hearing; ask him to bless and protect binoculars, telescopes, eyeglasses, magnifying glasses, hearing aids, and listening devices.
Heket:	She is an Egyptian Frog Goddess of childbirth and creation. In the shower, bathtub, or hot tub, she can be invoked by using a frog-shaped sponge or soap.
Helen:	Ask this Greek Moon Goddess of childbirth, love, and fertility to help you when doing Love Magick.
Hellith:	He is the Celtic God of the setting sun and protector of souls of the dead.
Hera:	Greek Goddess of women and their sexuality, including matrimony, she can be called upon when you are engaged in an e-mail or Internet courtship.
Hermes:	The Greek God of flocks and music and the divine messenger, he blesses and protects travelers.
Hertha, Herdda:	She is Celtic Goddess of fertility, Spring, the Earth, rebirth, and healing.
Hestia:	In the Greek tradition she is the Fire of the hearth, living in the center of every home. Call upon her to charge up your heaters, furnace, fireplace, woodstove, and other home heating appliances.

Horae: A group of Greek Goddesses representing the divine aspects of the natural order of the seasons, they are ideal gardening Goddesses who can be invited in when you are working in your yard or garden. Ask them to bless your gardening tools and machines such as your weed eater and rake. They are protective Goddesses for landscape workers, farmers, and horticultural specialists.

Hygeia: Greek Goddess of health, she might oversee holistic and magickal approaches to well-ness, too.

Hypnos: Mesmerizing Greek God of sleep and dreams; things such as self-hypnosis tapes and CDs, guided visualization tapes and CDs, and strobe lighting are all under his domain.

Inanna: This Sumerian Mother Goddess who brought civilization to humankind, went into the Underworld and lived to tell the tale. She is a Goddess of mining, homes built underground, basements, and underground parking lots.

Irene: Call upon this Greek Goddess of peace when you are doing global healing and Cyber Peace Magick.

Ishtar: She is the Babylonian Goddess of love, beauty, and war. Associated with Venus, the morning star, she is the perfect Goddess to call upon early in the morning to help you with your day.

Isis: She is the Egyptian Mother Goddess and the embodiment of femininity. Call her in when doing any kind of Cyber Magick.

Isong: Invoke this African Goddess of fertility when doing Cyber Love Magick.

Juno: This Roman Mother Goddess of matrimony, who rules over the entire reproductive cycle of women, is an e-mail Goddess.

Jupiter: Roman God of the light sky and wielder of thunderbolts, he is an Internet God of prosperity who rules online banking.

Kama, Kamadeva: Called the "Seed of Desire," he is a Hindu God of love.

Kernunnos, Cernunnos:
Celtic Father God of virility, prowess, and Nature, ask him to power up your Cyber Magick.

Kerridwen, Cerridwyn, Ceridwyn:
She is a Celtic Goddess of knowledge and wisdom who possessed the cauldron of inspiration. As such, she makes a great hot tub Goddess.

Krishna: He is a Hindu God of erotic delight and ecstasy.

Kwan Yin: She is an Asian Goddess of compassion and beauty.

Lakshmi: She is a Hindu Goddess of beauty and good fortune.

Llyr, Ler, Lir, Leur, Leer:

> He is the Sea God of music and King of the oceans.

Luchta or Lucta, Luchtaine:

> He is the Celtic Carpenter God and shield maker for the Tuatha De Dannan.

Lugh, Lleu, (Llew) Llaw Gyffes:

> Champion and Master of all arts, he is a Celtic Sun God who presides over natural energy sources such as solar power and all kinds of techno-tools. Also a God of poets, bards, smiths, and war, call upon him any time you are doing Cyber Magick.

Maat:

> She is the Egyptian Goddess of balance and truth.

Mabon, Mapon, Maponus:

> "The Divine Son" and "The Son of Light," he is a Celtic God of sex, love, magick, prophesy, and power. Lamps, lighting systems, and flashlights are all under his domain.

Macha (Maha):

> A Celtic war Goddess and powerful druidess of the Tuatha de Dannan, she is akin to Epona, the horse Goddess of wisdom, and associated with the horse, raven, and the crow. She is a Goddess suited to black cars and travel protection.

Manannan, Manannan ap Llyr, Manannan Mac Llyr:

> He is a shapeshifter, teacher, and Celtic God of magick, the sea, and travel. The Land of Promise, an Elysian island, is his home.

Math, Son of Mathonwy:

He is the Seasonal King and Welsh God of magick, wisdom, enchantment, and sorcery. Master of Cyber Magick, he is also the perfect God of foot massagers and footbaths.

Maya:

Hindu Goddess of creativity, she is ideal to call upon for help with your Cyber Magick. She reminds us that all things are illusion.

Medb, Maeve, Mab:

Called "Intoxication" or "Mead," she is the Celtic Warrior Queen and Goddess of sex, fertility, and sovereignty. She is also a protector Goddess of brewing establishments and bars.

Meditrina:

The Roman Goddess of medicine, wine, and health, she oversees surgical equipment and medical machines as well as medical supplies such as prescriptions.

Melpomene:

This Greek Muse of tragedies and songs of mourning is there when a cyber being ceases to exist and there is no chance of repair.

Mercury:

He is the Roman God of safe travel and communication, and in a cyber sense e-mail and cell phones.

Merlin, Myrddin: As a Cyber Wizard who can fix anything, he is an excellent divine power to call in when you are surfing on the Internet.

Mider, Midir: This Celtic Faery King, God of the Underworld, and consort to Etain is a bard and a chess player who is associated with the Isle of Man, the Faery hill of Bri Leith, the chess board, and game pieces. Call upon him when doing Cyber Faery Magick and when playing games on your computer.

Min: He is the Egyptian God of sex, fecundity, crops, and mechanical harvesting equipment and other farm machinery.

Modrona or Modron, Madrona, Matrona:
The Celtic Great Mother of Mabon (light), she can be called in to bless and protect anything that illuminates such as lamps.

Mokosh: She is the Slavic Great Goddess of the Earth.

Morgan Le Fey: She is a Faery Queen, sorceress, shapeshifter, and beautiful enchantress, perfect for Faery Cyber Magick.

Morgana: A shapeshifter and the Queen of Death, she is a Celtic Goddess of fertility and war who can help you reconfigure your system.

Morrigan or Morrigana:
"The Phantom Queen" or "Great Queen," and a sea Goddess, she is the Celtic Triple Goddess of War, who shapeshifts into a raven.

Morrigu: Called the Dark Gray Lady and Queen of the Sea, she is a Celtic Goddess of life, rebirth, and magick, who helps keep things flowing.

Mother Mary: The Christian archetype of the Mother Goddess, she gives birth to the son of the Divine through immaculate conception. Call her in when creating new businesses, crafting new ideas, and signing contracts.

Nantosuelta: As a Celtic River Goddess, she keeps the cyber power flowing.

Nemetona: Protectress of the sacred Drynemeton and personal Web sites, she is a Celtic Warrior Goddess of the oak groves and patron of thermal springs.

Nephthys: The Egyptian Goddess of dreams, divination, and hidden knowledge, she is a good choice to call upon when using the Internet for divination. There are many sites to chose from. Just type in "tarot" or "I Ching" for listings.

Nodens: Celtic God of dreams and sleep, he is the perfect God to call upon to bless and protect your alarm clock.

Norns: In Norse mythology, these three sisters, who control the destiny of everyone, are Urd, who creates patterns, Verdandi, who weaves them and gives them structure, and Sculd, who unravels them, throwing them back into the unmanifested. They can be called upon to bless and protect anything machine made or powered by electricity.

Nuada, Lludd, Nudd, Lludd Llaw Ereint:
    He is the Celtic good father, first king of Tara, consort to Fea, the war Goddess, and to Morrigan. Powerful chieftain God of thunder, kingship, rebirth, war, and wealth, he carries one of the Tuatha De Dannan's four treasures: the sword from Findias.

Nwyvre: Celtic God of space and the firmament, and consort to Arianrhod, he is the ideal God to bless and protect space shuttles, space ships, space probes, satellites, and other space vehicles. He is also a good choice for help with UFO and contact experiences.

Odin: The Norse All-Father of wisdom and inspiration is an excellent cyber protector and power God.

Ogma, Ogmios: Called "The Binder," he is the Celtic God of eloquence, knowledge, and literature who invented the Ogham. Call on him when you are downloading fonts, e-books, and current events from the Internet.

Omamama: The Cree ancestral Goddess of beauty, fertility, gentleness, and love; you can call her in to help you with cyber love spells.

Oshun: She is the African Goddess of love, pleasure, beauty, and dancing.

Osiris: He is the Egyptian Father God of civilization and rebirth who can be called in when using techno-tools.

Pan: Greek Nature God of lust, love, play, and pleasure; ask him in when you are playing games on your computer or TV, especially sexy ones!

Pi-Hsai Yuan-Chin:
A Chinese Goddess of childbirth, she brings health and good fortune to the newborn and protection to the mother.

Polyhymnia: She is the Greek Muse of hymns, mimic art, and harmony.

Psyche: This Greek Goddess of love can inspire your cyber spells.

Ra: As an Egyptian solar God with a detachable eye, he is ideal for blessing and protecting all kinds of cameras and solar power systems.

Rhiannon: Called Queen Mother, Queen Mare, or the Great Queen, she is helpful for all travel spells, especially Air travel.

Robur: He is a Celtic Forest King and Monadic tree God of the forests, particularly oaks. Call to him whenever you knock on wood three times.

Rosemerta: A Celtic Goddess of virtual flowers, especially roses, her qualities are fertility, beauty, love, and plenty.

Sadv: She is a very ancient Celtic Deer Goddess of the forests and Nature, and Mother to Oisin, the poet. Call her power to you by chanting her name when you see deer-sign. These can be either outdoors or on signs, on TV, statues in yards, and the like.

Saga: Norse Goddess of poetry who is the ideal Goddess of all archives (both printed and computerized); call upon her to bless your computer files, video tape and CD collections, and file cabinets.

Shakti: The Great Hindu Mother Goddess, who embodies feminine energy; call upon her to add the feminine touch to your cyber spells.

Shiva:	The Hindu God of creation who embodies masculine energy; invite his powers into your cyber space when you need to take strong positive action.
Sinann (Sinand):	The Goddess of the River Shannon, she is a cyber Goddess of power and wisdom. The White Trout and the Salmon of Knowledge are probably incarnations of Sinann.
Sirona:	Celtic sun and star Goddess; call upon her when you enter cyberspace to bless, guide, and protect you. She is also an ideal Goddess to help you get off the grid and on solar energy.
Smertullos:	The Preserver and Lord of Protection, a Celtic God of the abyss and the unmanifested, he lords over computer recycle bins and the "empty trash" option on your e-mail.
Soma:	A Hindu God of inspiration with 27 wives, this being might rightly oversee those people who choose polyamory as a lifestyle.
Sucellos:	He is the Celtic River God and twin to the Dagda, shapeshifter, and God of fertility and death.
Sulis:	As a Celtic Goddess of healing and warm springs, call her in when you are hot-tubbing or taking a bath or shower.
Taliesin:	Son of Celtic Mother Goddess Cerridwen, he is a poet, prophet, and bard. Call on him when you crave creative inspiration.
Tarvos:	The Celtic God of the seasons who takes the form of a bull; you can call upon him during a bullish stock market.

Terpsichore:	The Greek muse of dancing and music, particularly the choral song; all kinds of electronic music come under her domain.
Thalia:	The festive Greek Muse of comedy and idyllic poetry; invite her into your home when you play comedy movies on your VCR or DVD player.
Thor:	As a Norse God of thunder and protector from chaos, his techno-tool is a pneumatic hammer.
Thoth:	He is the Egyptian God of writing, moon God, and master cyber magician.
Tlazolteotl:	She is a Peruvian Goddess of love who can be useful when doing cyber love spells.
Triana:	This is the triple Celtic Goddess: Sun-Ana, Earth-Ana, and Moon-Ana. Also the Goddess of healing, knowledge, higher love, and wisdom.

Turanna, Turan (originally an Etruscan Goddess, later Italian):
She is known as "the Good Feary" of peace and love.

Tyr:	Norse God of war and justice; call upon him when doing cyber spells for justice and legal matters.
Urania:	As the Greek Muse of astronomy, things such as telescopes, camera lenses, and space are under her domain.
Var:	She is a Scandinavian love Goddess who is helpful when doing cyber love spells.

Venus: She is a Roman Goddess of love and sexuality who is ideal to call upon when doing Cyber Love Magick.

Vesta: She is a Roman Goddess of Fire and the hearth who can be called upon when you turn on your electric heater and electric stove.

Viviana, Vivian: Her name means life, so any time you push the power button, you can call her to bless, guide, and protect you and your cyber sorcery. She is the Celtic Goddess of love, birth, mothers, childbirth, and children.

Voluspa: As a Norse Goddess who is known as a famous seer, she is the ideal Goddess to guide consulting firms, financial advisers, and stock brokers.

Zeus: The powerful leader of the Greek Gods of Olympus, Zeus makes a great All-Father stock market God.

As Above, So Below— Cyber Components and Focals

Witches often use the phrase "as above, so below." This means that all things in the world have a mirror somewhere else. For example, the starfish in the sea mirrors the star in the sky, an atom is a miniature solar system, and so forth.

This aphorism reminds us that balance is a key ingredient in our Witchery. Thus the initial phrase is often coupled with "as within, so without," especially when talking about our magickal pursuits. Whatever we're doing magickally should be mirrored substantively to honor our spirits and keep us honest. This symmetry is nothing less than essential for maintaining our role as co-creators in our destiny.

"As above, so below; as within, so without" gives us a major clue as to how to update our components so they better suit this brave new world in which we live. As we look at these concepts in our magickal methodology, the Cyber Witch first considers placement (the below, the without, the here and now). Exactly how is the world seeing or thinking about an item or date? Next, the Cyber Witch looks within and above the higher Self and Spirit to apply that construct metaphysically. Keep this basic process in mind as you read this chapter.

The Cyber Witch Broom Closet

Being forward-thinkers and flying off to check out the latest gadgets, Cyber Witches don't necessarily stick to the standard components and correspondence lists. Many of our components not only have traditional value, but can also be applied in the virtual world. This section examines various items that can be applied in just that manner.

Many of the items in our Cyber Witch broom closet are things we use at home. Over the years, most Witches collect a number of the tools of the trade, such as stones, incenses, herbs, or gadgets. As American Cyber Witches and Pagan authors, our waking reality may be a little different than yours, so apply liberal amounts of personal vision to this section.

Consider creating a correspondence list of your own. After all, everyone has personal favorites when it comes to things such as music, appliances, gadgets, colors, scents, crystals, and symbols. Use what works for you. Trust your intuition and allow your spirit and heart to guide you.

User-Friendly Focals

You may be amazed at what we consider a user-friendly focal. Don't be alarmed—it's all pretty self-explanatory. Some of it, we realize, is a little bizarre, but keep an open mind. Everything from herbs, spices, plants, and edibles to crystals, radios, rototillers, and digital cameras, as well as common household items such as slotted spoons and blenders, can be used as focals.

In spellcraft, ritual, divination, and charm creation, most magickal folk turn to specific components that become focals and helpmates to the process. The following types of focals help focus your magickal power:

✳ Auditory focals: Things you hear, such as voices, music, drumming, waterfalls, and bird song.

✳ Gustatory focals: Things you taste, such as food and drink.

✳ Intuitive focals: Things you intuit, such as talismans, certain jewelry, and medicine bags.

✳ Kinesthetic focals: Things you touch, such as people, animals, plants, trees, leaves, soil, seeds, and fabrics.

✳ Olfactory focals: Things you smell, such as flowers, incense, smudge, scented candles, and scented oils.

✳ Visual focals: Things you see, such as photographs, symbols, paintings, books, flashing lights, and Goddess and God figurines.

You probably noticed that a lot of user-friendly focals fall into several categories. For example, a rose can be used as a visual (you look at it), olfactory (you smell it), kinesthetic (you touch it), intuitive (it evokes certain intuitions and psychic abilities), and sometimes even a gustatory focal (you can eat it). A car radio can be used as an auditory (you hear it), kinesthetic (you touch the knobs, the cassettes, the CDs), and intuitive focal (certain music can evoke certain abilities that enhance ritual and magick).

Focals also represent the four Elements of Earth, Air, Fire, and Water, and their directions of North, East, South, and West. Everything in ritual and magick, absolutely *everything*, plays into the elements and their inherent powers. Again, some focals represent more than one Element. For example, a clothes dryer is associated with Fire/South and Air/East. Always keep in mind that the fifth Element is Spirit—that's you the practitioner. You are the one who plugs it in and pushes the on/off button.

Techno-Mechanical and Household Items/Tools

What would a book on Cyber Magick be without a ready list of cyber-oriented components? To keep things zipping, we thought we'd plug things in and flip out some old-school Witches, and intrigue a few new-school ones. Suffice to say, we are shaped by our culture and current technologies. So it's time to update your magickal files and have fun!

Our ancestors were very pragmatic. If the symbolic value of something worked, they put it to good use. They certainly didn't have all the gadgets we have today, but you can bet that cigarette lighter would have quickly been used to light a candle or sacred fire.

We decided not to include brand names when considering both traditional and modern components for obvious legal and practical reasons. However, when you walk through any supermarket or retail outlet, be mindful that the names for each product have been carefully chosen and contrived to have a specific conscious and subconscious effect on you, the consumer. That very same effect can empower your ritual and spellcrafting when you use the product for matching magickal purposes!

Let's create a fictitious example. If a manufacturer creates and produces Pure Soap, that item is perfectly suited for magickal purification or for any magick focused on pure intention. In particular, it might become part of a preritual purification bath! So don't limit your search for cyber components to superficials. Consider all dimensions of the items you're considering before determining the best symbolic application.

Review the following list of techno-mechanical and household items. Consider applying their practical powers to your Cyber Magick each and every day.

Air-Conditioner: Cold contracts things, so you can use your air-conditioner to contract your energetic space, to be more introspective. You can do this in the car, at home, or at the office. Associated with Air and Water, air-conditioning can also be used to air out your emotions, to chill out, reduce physical stress, or cool off when you are angry. So be cool!

Bathtub: Associated with the element of Water and the West, bathtubs can be used for ritual baths, which are taken in preparation for doing ritual or magick. Also, the bathtub makes great cauldron or scrying tool.

Battery: Power packs, as are fuel cells, areassociated with Fire and the South. They are used to power your techno-tools.

Blender: A mix between a modern athame and cauldron, the blender stirs things up. It is perfect for increasing the energy in potions and gives whole new meaning to "whipping something up." Use the blender to blend ideas, realities, and cultures and to improve cooperation.

Bread Maker: Associated with Fire and Earth; a tool for making ritual bread, rolls, and pizza. Breadsticks, decorated with runes, make handy edible wands. Put a pinch of herbs that are pleasing to your taste buds and your magickal purpose in your breads. For example, add crushed almonds or a dash of almond extract to the bread for fertility or prosperity spells. Use the buzzer on the bread maker as a signal to call in your favorite prosperity Goddess and God.

Calculator: Associated with Fire and Earth, it can be used for prosperity spells, reducing debt, and setting figures and calculating dates for attaining personal goals.

Camera or Digital Camera:

A picture is worth a thousand words! Photographs capture good times, favorite people and places, and your deepest wishes and are excellent focals in magick because they carry great power. A photograph is like a moment of time, locked in place, encapsulated, if you will. You can work magick off of that moment. Now, with digital cameras, you can take a photo, and then transform it into just about anything you can imagine—as long as you can find the graphics! Talk about magickal power, not to mention instant gratification! Some people will not allow themselves to be photographed because they feel it takes away their power. It's important to respect their wishes.

Car, Truck, or Van:

Our mechanical horses, oxen, llamas, mules, and donkeys are our cars, trucks, and vans. They contain the Elements of Earth, Air, Fire, and Water, with the driver representing the element of Spirit. Your automobile may also carry the name of one of your power animals such as "mustang" or "ram."

CD Player: Music is pure manna to the Cyber Witch. A body, mind, and spirit magickal tool, you can use certain selections of music to greatly enhance your rituals and spells.

CD: These disks are circular and symbols of the Goddess. They can also represent the Wheel of the Year. You can share music by recycling old CDs instead of throwing them away. You can sell them to used bookstores, donate them to your local libraries, clubs, and schools, or give them to someone who would appreciate them. You can also charge old CDs with specific types of magickal energy, put witchy stickers on them, and paint Goddess and God symbols on them, such as stars and moons, to use them as focals.

Cellular Phone: As one of the most powerful modern cyber tools, you can use your cell phone to send your spells over the "connect" key (especially those for improved networking). Associated with Air (communication) and the East, these are very personal cyber wands, often used to contact loved ones or people that can help during emergencies and dire circumstances.

Chainsaw: Representing the Fire Element, this is a modern athame of the deadliest kind. It's the Cyber Magick tool of the Celtic hunter God Esus, the woodcutter.

Clock or Watch: A tool for magickal timing, you can set your watch or clock to match the nature of your spellcrafting. The following are basic numerological qualities of the hours:

1. Oneness, beginnings, independence, and creativity.

2. Partnership, the blending of two Elements into one, and working with others.

3. The threefold nature of divinity, a number of Divine power, communication, expansion, and luck.

4. Foundations, the four sacred directions, construction, productivity, and organization.

5. A magickal number of the five-pointed star (pentagram), curiosity, travel, change, and resourcefulness.

6. Home, family, children, pet companions, creative love, nourishment, and beauty.

7. Divine wisdom, the seven chakras, birth and rebirth, and spiritual faith.

8. Business, material prosperity, infinity, reward, success, and leadership.

9. Universal compassion, tolerance, completion, and humanitarianism.

10. Refer to 1 (1 + 0 = 1).

11. Either 11, which is a master number(a number of intuition, telepathy, spiritual healing, and psychic abilities), or refer to 2 (1 + 1 = 2).

12. Refer to 3 (1 + 2 = 3).

Clothes Dryer: Associated with the Air and Fire Elements, the dryer represents the directions of East and South. Using the clothes dryer for Cyber Magick gives a whole new meaning to the expression, "Oh, dry up!"

Coffee Maker: A great Cyber Magick tool because it combines all four elements: Earth (pot, machine, and coffee beans), Air (the pungent aroma), Fire (power on and heating device), and Water (the water and coffee). The pot makes the perfect cauldron for your morning ritual potion of a cup of hot java.

Coffee Bean Grinder:

A must-have tool for Cyber Witches, especially those with a morning coffee ritual. With its sharp blade, it's a mechanical athame associated with the South and Fire. Keep a second one for grinding powders for potions.

Colander: Good for straining negativity out of something without losing its essence, the colander is a kitchen Cyber Witch's tool for releasing emotions such as anger and self-pity. Shaking the excess water out when draining pasta, for example, can be used to represent filtering out excess emotions (water).

Computer:

* *Floppy disks* are portable and filled with information. think of them as four-cornered archives of knowledge. They can be used as Watchtower markers at the four directions of a magick Circle.

* *The hard drive* has amazing storage capacity and is akin to a sacred well for preserving knowledge. It is associated with the Earth element and the North.

* *The keyboard* represents the creative flow. You think about something, you type it, and then you see it—talk about manifesting power! Certain keys can be used for Cyber Magick. For example, the "Delete" key for banishing, the "Enter" key for entering your magickal Cyber Circle, and the "Shift" key for shifting between the ordinary and magickal worlds. You can use a miniature besom (Witch's broom) or small paintbrush to remove dust between keys on your keyboard. While doing this, chant this simple clearing spell, "Dust be gone, sweep it clean. Bless the Mother, keep her Green."

* *The mouse* is akin to a magickal wand. As you move and click it, it takes you wherever you want to go on the Internet. It "points" the way to power and can be used for directional focus when doing spellwork on your computer screen. With screen savers, you can now change the mouse arrow into a starfish, skin-diver, and so forth, depending on the screensaver motif and graphics.

✳ *The screen* is a large eye of knowledge and a light-filled tool for visualization and stretching your imagination. Through the screen, you can view the true nature, the soul, of your computer. The words and graphics beam out at you, and you look in at them.

✳ *The tower* represents the Earth Element, the North, and houses your drives, disks, CD-ROM, power button or switch, and other component parts of the computer.

✳ Many computers come equipped with a small *wand,* a tool associated with Air and the East. The wand is used to touch the screen to give commands.

Dishwasher: A modern hotsprings for implements of the Goddess such as the plates, bowls, glasses, cups, spoons, fork, and knives. They are all-around symbols of the Goddess. The altar is the Lady's Table. You can clean your potion containers in the dishwasher, running them through the entire cycle, and turning on the heat and dry cycle. This sterilizes the containers.

Electric Can Opener:
Modern day athames, representing Fire and the South, most electric can openers have sharpeners so you can use them to sharpen your bolline and athame.

Electric Drill: Representing Fire and Earth, the electric drill (and pneumatic hammer) has replaced the hammer.

Electric Fan: With the powers of Air, associated with the East, blow what you want into your life, and blow what you don't want out of your life, with your electric fan.

Food Processor: This is the Cyber Witch's cauldron extraordinaire! It can chop and mix just about anything. Talk about the power to stir things up!

Freezer: As can the Isa rune in the Futhark, the cold can also be used to slow things down or stop them. It's a great Cyber Magick tool for freezing troublemakers and problems out of your life.

Hair Dryer: Associated with Air and Fire (heat), it can be used to blow that lover right into your hair, and heat things up, too!

Heater: Representing Fire (and Air, if it has a fan), when doing Cyber Magick, position your heater in the South (or southeast) point of your Magick Circle.

Hot Tub: The cauldron of the Goddess—well, at least for these two Cyber Witches! Perfect for skyclad Moon Magick with your lover!

Juicer: A must cyber ritual tool for all Cyber Witches who are veggie and fruit lovers and who are into fresh and healthy potions. The juicer blade (Fire) and the juice (Water within the fruit) make a tasty combination of Elements!

Lamp: A candle without the dangers of a flame, the lamp can be used to represent the Fire Element and the South Quarter, not to mention help you see what you're doing. A good reading lamp is a must for all knowledgeable Cyber Witches.

Lawn Mower: Gas and push mowers, representing Fire (blade) and Earth (the mower body), are the power techno-tools for the Harvest God.

Memory Chip: A symbol of Earth, you can punch a hole in a chip and put it on your key chain to "remember" what you need to do that day.

Oven (conventional and microwave):
A cyber tool that represents Fire and the South. Use your oven to heat your magick up and get things cooking! Keep in mind that a microwave oven does take some of the power out of your potion or Cyber Magick foods.

Pens and Pencils: As small and readily available Cyber Witch wands, they are symbols of communication, associated with the East and the Air Element.

Plug-In Room Scents:
Element of Air, plus the properties of the specific scent. For example, vanilla sweetens your spellcasting and rituals, whereas lavender helps you stay relaxed and calm.

Pots and Pans: You can use these modern versions of cauldrons and vessels to simmer a potion or two!

Radio: Represents Air and communication. Radio music, talk shows, and news on the radio can all be used to convey emotion and intent in spellcasting and ritual. You can easily tape record or play radio music to fit your magick.

Refrigerator: Associated with Earth, Air, and Water, use refrigerators to keep all your perishable focals, including food and potions, fresh and lively.

Rototiller: As a cyber tool of the Earth God and Goddess, it represents Fire/South and Earth/North.

Scissors: Representing Fire/South, scissors are a form of athame, used to cut things loose and for separating. They can also be used for starting business ventures (cutting the ribbon).

Stereo Receiver: Power on this cyber tool of Fire. Put on the perfect CD or musical program to amplify your cyber spells and rituals.

Stove: Associated with Fire/South, the stove is handy for cooking potions. To attract prosperity into your home using basic feng shui, put a mirror behind the burners of your stove. This doubles them visually, and thus doubles the wealth that comes into your home.

Straining Spoon: Put this in a window or on a wall facing outward to strain out unwanted energies.

Tabletop Fountains:
They represent Water/West, the Goddess, the well, and cauldron, small fountains now come in all sizes and colors, sometimes with colored lights. Use a fountain to bring the relaxing feeling of Nature indoors.

Tape Recorder: This powerful techno-tool can be used to store words of power, initiation ceremonies, spellcasting invocations, prayers, blessings, and special music.

Telephone: Representing Air/East and an immense web of networks, the telephone is a tool for keeping in touch with friends and family and making connections such as hooking up to the Internet.

Telephone Answering Machine:

Associated with Air/East and communication, these little machines have greatly improved the quality of life, especially for those of us who work at home. Now you have the power to choose when you do and do not want to answer your telephone. You can use your answering machine message as a charm. Use rhyming words or phrases and an inviting tone of voice to entice that certain someone to leave a message!

Toy:

Besides working on your inner child, each toy has specific potential. For example, a snow globe might represent the Water Element in the western Quarter of your sacred space, whereas a top could be specially decorated to spin your magickal energy!

Toys such as singing and talking animals can be used as power animal representations, for example, robotic dogs and cats. Remote control trucks and cars can help you get where you want in cyber spellcasting. Computer games can take you just about everywhere. Be sure to put a little more playtime in your life. It's been the experience of these two moms that children, as well as adults, love to use toys in rituals and magick making. It adds to the fun in life.

TV:

A blank TV screen functions perfectly as a scrying tool. You can also invoke all the Elements on the screen when it's on, especially when you use certain videos and programs you tape yourself.

Vacuum Cleaner: Representing Air and Fire, this techno-tool of purification can be used to suck up unwanted dirt and energies.

VCR: The true cyber tool of the power of personal selection, your VCR allows you to control your personal space and tune into what you want. Cyber paradise is TV with no commercials. Your VCR can take you there!

Video Camera: A visual cyber tool that can help you create powerful magick. For example, with the help of a friend, you can film yourself in your favorite place in Nature and play it when you are feeling stressed out and disconnected. You can film your family and friends having fun, and play it when you are feeling lonely or sad.

Washing Machine: A symbol of Water and the Goddess, use your washing machine to clean up things in your life.

Wire, Cord, Plug, and Outlet: Like umbilical cords to energy, these keep our cyber tools connected and powered and keep the cyber juices flowing.

Turn on the Lights!

Lighting devices represent Fire and the South. When you use your computer and appliances for making magick, you can use a lamp, a small light box, miniature houses, other decorations with small light bulbs inside, Christmas lights, as well as silk flowers fitted with small lights, decorative lighted strings of plastic pumpkins, elves, snowmen, stars, and flowers. You can use a small penlight or flashlight during rituals and spellworking. For illuminating your altar, use a small lamp (even a portable book lamp). You can change the color of your lamp bulbs to match the desired symbolism.

Most Cyber Witches still like using traditional candles for magick. There is something about a lit candle that sets the tone for making magick the way nothing else can. Before you use your candles, smudge them with purifying smoke or wash them in cool salt water to get rid of unwanted energies. Usually you burn candles all the way down. Make certain you have a fireproof holder and surface where the candle can burn down in complete safety. Keep the candle flame away from flammable items such as curtains, scented oils, paper, and upholstery. When you don't have time to let the candle burn all the way down, or you don't want it to, put it out with a candle snuffer. You can always light it the next day and burn it down. There are also small spell candles with holders readily available at your local grocery store, on the Internet, and in Witch shops. These are handy for spellcasting because they burn down quickly.

Candles come in all colors. The idea is to match the candle color to your spellcasting or ritual. Here is a list of colors and their basic magickal qualities:

White: Moon power, communication with the Goddess or God, Divine inspiration, protection, guidance, truth, motivation.

Black: Divination, magickal power, getting rid of negativity, ending relationships, the shadow self.

Gray/Silver: Mastery, divination, Dream Magick, wisdom, merging, moon energy, ancestor contact, purification, astral travel.

Blue: Healing, higher wisdom, clearing out negative energies, loyalty, protection, travel.

Gold/Yellow: Personal power, creativity, sun power, increase, mental agility, attraction, teaching, learning.

Green: Fertility, growth, prosperity, healing, good luck, shapeshifting, fertility, regeneration.

Purple/Violet: Spiritual awareness, balance, psychic ability, ancestral power, nobility, protection, dreaming.

Pink/Rose: Love, romance, friendship, kinship, children, relaxation.

Red: Power, sexuality, passion, creativity, vitality, action, courage, rebirth.

Orange: Success, prosperity, healing, meditation, justice, constructive action.

Brown: Earth power, healing, grounding, the harvest, animal protection, family, home, common sense.

Turn on the Music!

Music turns on our emotions, our desires. Its rhythm and cadence soothes the savage beast in all of us. It is a potent salve for anger, frustration, and stress. It's healing! After all, you almost always feel better after listening to music you enjoy.

Most Cyber Witches are music lovers. They know that the power of song and symphony can be used in rituals, in spellcrafting, and for inspiration. Today, with music literally at your fingertips with the push of a button, there are so many sources for tunes. You can turn on the CD or tape player or radio, slip a CD into the CD-ROM on your computer, and find tunes on cable TV.

When doing ritual and spellcrafting, listening to a certain kind of music, or a specific song or musical piece can help you focus. The music can empower and move you into an altered state of consciousness, one more conducive to merging with the Divine.

Music influences your body, mind, and spirit. Through trial and error, you can learn to match certain music with successful magick. Music has a more dramatic influence when it moves you emotionally, so select tunes that you love for your cyber spells and rituals.

Cyber Crystals and Stones

Being part magpie, Cyber Witches appreciate the power and beauty of crystals and gemstones. Small portable items such as these are easily carried or stored wherever the energy is most needed. Also, wearing jewelry set with stones transmits their powerful qualities, especially when the stone makes contact with your skin. Here is a list of a few of our favorite stones and their magickal uses:

Agate: Use this to protect all forms of communication, from your interpersonal discussions to phone calls, e-mail, and chat-room participation. A nice balancing stone to hold in your hand when surfing the Internet and checking out Web sites.

Amber: It's not *really* a stone, but we are including it here because it is often used as a stone in magick. Amber is a tree resin. It's considered a healer's stone that captures sickness and wards off negativity. Keep amber near your techno-tools to maintain their health and keep them in good working order. Amber acts as a powerful energy shield when worn over the heart area. It's a good choice to hold in your receptive hand (the one you don't eat with) when downloading mellow tunes on the Internet or listening to and meditating to soft music.

Amethyst:

Put this powerful dreaming and psychic stone under your pillow when vision is needed. Place a small flat amethyst geode about a foot away from your computer tower to keep it running smoothly. You can put small tumbled or raw pieces of hematite, malachite, citrine, and clear quartz on top of the geode. The geode will constantly clear any unwanted energy out of the stones you place on top of it. You can then use the hematite, malachite, citrine, and clear quartz pieces for cyber magick.

Carnelian:

As a stone with solar cyber power, use it for protection, courage, focus, and motivation, to enhance sexuality and creativity, and to tap into past lives.

Citrine:

The mind stone of mental quickness and insight, you can use citrine for Dream Magick, personal empowerment, shapeshifting, and to dispel negativity.

Clear Quartz:

Because quartz is used as an energy source itself, it fits in with the techno-magick motif.

Just about everything has crystals, from your watch to your credit cards. There are crystals all around you, which means you are constantly being influenced by their energy fields. A master stone in magick, quartz crystals can be used for healing, divination, meditation, shapeshifting, creativity, higher consciousness, purification, protection, and balancing energy. Clear quartz crystals make particularly powerful Circle markers. Use four different crystals to mark the directions of North, East, South, and West of your magick Cyber Circle. Charge them with the Element they represent.

Diamond:

A traditional stone of strength, endurance, healing, empowerment, inspiration, protection, prosperity, and clarity; it's clear why so many handfasting, engagement, and wedding rings have diamonds on them. It's also no wonder that so many industrial tools use diamond heads for exact cutting. This stone shines with all of the colors of the rainbow, which means it contains all of the colors and their inherent magickal qualities.

Emerald:

A soft healing stone that is easy to scratch and crack. It encourages love, emotional and sexual balance, patience, and personal growth. Emerald can be used for meditation, prayer, and raising consciousness.

Garnet:

To encourage friendship and faithfulness, wear a garnet ring. Other magickal qualities ascribed to this stone are strength, protection, virility, trust, balance, and good luck.

Hematite:

Because of its iron oxide nature, its density, and its weight, hematite makes the perfect Cyber Magick stone. It's akin to a natural grounding wire in the form of a stone. Hold a piece of tumbled hematite in your hand after working on your computer or when you are around many machines to ground your energies. Wear hematite when you are feeling light-headed or scattered when working. It will help you come back down to earth and focus on the task at hand. You can also use it to reduce stress, for protection, and to boost self-esteem.

Jade:

A powerful and sensual stone for love and sex magick, jade is considered the concentrated essence of love. It dispels negativity and calms your nerves. Jade's magickal qualities include protection, prosperity, purification, meditation, harmony, and longevity.

Malachite:

It can be used for healing, shapeshifting, communicating with power animals, Faery Magick, peaceful sleep, and visions. It encourages prosperity (especially in business) and can be used for protection and tissue regeneration. Malachite helps to neutralize unhealthy energies from computers, machines, and the like.

Moonstone:

A sacred stone of the Goddess, it brings good fortune, true love, and fruitfulness. Use moonstone to enhance your intuition and for divination, Moon Magick, fertility spells, lunar healing, receptivity, and enhanced creativity in the arts.

Rose Quartz: This stone can be used to balance your emotions, to attract friends, and for Love Magick. It encourages inspiration, forgiveness, faith, fertility, tolerance, and compassion.

Ruby: A personal empowerment stone that amplifies energies. Use it to activate the life force. Helpful for building magickal power and strength, the ruby can also be used for protection, insight, creativity, passion, and attracting friends and business associates.

Smokey Quartz A healing and grounding stone. Use smokey quartz to get rid of unwanted habits and build healthy patterns in your life. You can use it to dispel radiation when working with techno-tools and doing Cyber Magick. Keep a piece of smokey quartz handy. When you feel ill at ease, are fatigued, or suffer from low self-esteem, pick the stone up and hold it in your power hand for at least five minutes. You will feel more centered, stronger, and more yourself.

Spicing Up Your Cyber Space

In times of old, magick and healing both came out of one's pantry. Because one of the Cyber Witch's mottos is, "If it's not broken, don't fix it," we go to our pantry to spice up our Cyber Magick.

Sticking with the "as within, so without" concept, bring the outdoors in and use the beneficial powers of Nature's gifts for more successful Cyber Magick rituals and spells. Herbs, flowers, fruits, trees, plants, and other treasures of Nature all have inherent magickal qualities. They absorb

energies from the Elements and from the earth, sun, and moon.
They store this vital power. Knowledgeable Cyber Witches
know how to tap into this power.

Your sense of smell is the sense closest tied to your
memory. It has a direct effect on you, so using a certain
scented oil or particular kind of incense is likened to playing a
specific song each time you do magick. The scent, as does the
music, triggers a magickal response from you. Remember to
select scents that empower you—ones that you love to smell!

Scented oils can be very potent, so take precautions when
you use them. Make a skin patch test before using any oil on
your skin. If you have any adverse reactions, immediately
discontinue using it. Always dilute essential oils with a carrier oil.

You can dab scented oils on your skin, on your altar tools,
and on the fronts of appliances. Be careful not to put oils on
computer keyboard, tower, printer, or near the innards of
appliances, heaters, or on anything mechanical that gets
hot. To sweeten your kitchen, you can put a few drops of
lemon-scented oil or vanilla extract into a small pan of boiling water to release the fragrance.

To charge your oils, herbs, flowers, and other focals, hold
the item in your hands, and imagine a bright beam or wave
of light moving from your hands into the focal, empowering
it. Imagine using the focal for successful cyber ritual and
spellcrafting. Do this for a minute or so before using the
item.

The following list of scents, herbs, flowers, and the like,
plus their magickal qualities, can be used as a jumping off
point for spicing up your Cyber Magick.

Alfalfa: Prosperity, sustenance, healing.

Anise: Purification, healing, protection,
                  dreaming.

Almond:	Prosperity, wisdom.
Amber:	Love, happiness, strength.
Apple:	Love, happiness, good luck, Faery Magick.
Apricot:	Love, creativity, friendship.
Balsam Fir:	Prosperity, mental clarity.
Basil:	Protection, purification, wealth, faithfulness.
Bay:	Protection, purification, healing, dreaming, divination, and repels negativity.
Benzoin:	Purification, prosperity (Benzoin tincture can be used to preserves oils).
Caraway:	Love, passion.
Carnation:	Protection, blessing, strength.
Catnip:	Cat Magick, attraction, friendship, healing, dreaming, consecration.
Cayenne:	Increases your cyber magickal power, healing.
Cedar:	Money, healing, protection, purification, calming, comforting, and strengthening.
Chamomile:	Success, love, purification, peace, harmony, healing, Faery Magick, Cat Magick.
Cinnamon:	Psychic power, protection, love, creativity.

Cinquefoil:	Protection, prosperity.
Clove:	Protection, prosperity, purification, love, visions.
Clover:	Beauty, healing, good luck, visions, Faery Magick, Cat Magick.
Coriander:	Longevity, love, serenity, harmony.
Daisy:	Blessings, happiness, love, joy, Faery Magick.
Dandelion:	Purification, divination.
Dill:	Love, dreaming, protection.
Dragon's blood:	Love, protection, exorcism.
Echinacea:	Strength, healing, protection.
Eucalyptus:	Healing, protection.
Garlic:	Protection, courage, healing.
Geranium:	Love, fertility, protection, balancing.
Ginger:	Prosperity, love, power, success, healing, strength.
Ginseng:	Desire, love, longevity, healing.
Grape:	Money, fertility, mental clarity.
Honeysuckle:	Prosperity, love, protection, relaxation.
Hyacinth:	Love, happiness, protection, success.

Ivy:	Protection, good luck.
Jasmine:	Love, seduction, dreaming.
Juniper:	Purification, protection against harm and theft, love.
Lavender:	Love, peace, purification, protection, calming, balancing.
Lemon:	Purification, love, healing, blessings, friendship, clarity.
Lilac:	Exorcism, protection, love, harmony, memory, concentration.
Mandrake:	Courage, protection, fertility, potency.
Marigold:	Justice, love, dreaming, renewal, prophesy, healing.
Marjoram:	Healing, protection, fertility, love, happiness.
Mint:	Passion, protection, travel, luck, exorcism, healing, clarity, memory.
Mugwort:	Visions, astral travel, protection, dreaming, divination.
Mullein:	Purification, protection, courage.
Myrrh:	Consecration, protection, purification.
Nettle:	Healing, protection, strength.
Nutmeg:	Visions, divination, clairvoyance, dreaming.
Onion:	Healing, protection.

Orange:	Love, divination, luck, fertility.
Parsley:	Healing, vitality.
Patchouli:	Prosperity, passion, fertility, attraction.
Pine:	Fertility, prosperity, exorcism, protection, purification.
Poppy:	Fertility, prosperity, creativity, dreaming.
Rose:	Love, luck, divination, protection, peace, friendship, strength.
Rosemary:	Protection, healing, passion, clarity, purification, courage.
Saffron:	Healing, passion, divination, prosperity.
Sage:	Wisdom, fertility, protection, purification, longevity, healing.
Sandalwood:	Protection, healing, purification.
Sesame:	Prosperity, passion, love, lust, fertility, Bird Magick.
Saint-Johnis-wort:	Healing, purification, protection, dreaming.
Strawberry:	Love, luck, passion, gifts, joy, happiness, Faery Magick.
Sunflower:	Fertility, prosperity, blessings, Bird Magick.
Thyme:	Dreaming, courage, healing, protection, purification.

Valerian:	Love, sleep, purification, healing.
Vanilla:	Passion, love, harmony, attraction.
Vervain:	Consecration, purification, dreaming, protection, good luck.
Violet:	Protection, good luck, love, healing.
Willow:	Healing, blessings, divination.
Yarrow:	Healing, love, courage, protection, divination.

*Note: For those who are bothered by incense smoke, there are smokeless incenses and essential oil diffusers.

Magickal Cyber Foods and Tasty Potions

Magickal foods and potions can be used to empower your cyber spells and rituals. Spells with food, good food, are always more fun! Edible foods and tasty potions make for great magick because you literally internalize and digest the energy they contain when you consume them.

When you prepare magickal foods, focus on the magickal qualities you want to "cook" into the food. Keep your magickal goal in mind during the entire culinary process—the planning, cooking, and eating. The more you do this, the stronger the magickal power of the food. Have fun and decorate your foods with magickal symbols, runes, or your initials.

Tasty potions for drinking can be made with a mixture of ingredients such as fruits, spices, or herbal teas. Today many of the items used for preparing potions are techno-tools, for example, blenders, juicers, stoves, and coffee grinders.

When you make your potions, just as with your magickal foods, be sure to charge them with energy. Do this by focusing your mind on the qualities you want the potion to have. Use focused intention plus the energies of the potion's ingredients to build the energy of the potion. Charge the ingredients through your willful intent, through your touch, and through the heat of your hands. Actually imagine putting your magickal goal into the potion itself. Then further empower the potion by saying,

> Great cyber powers that be
>
> Charge this potion with divine energy
>
> In space, on Earth, sky, and sea
>
> As I will, so shall it be!

Stir together these tasty potions. They will certainly sweeten up your Cyber Magick!

Power-On Potion

1/8 cup chilled papaya juice

1/4 cup chilled grape juice

1/2 cup chilled raspberries or strawberries

1 cup raspberry or strawberry yogurt

1/8 cup ice water

Put all the ingredients in the blender, one at a time, dedicating each one to a favorite Goddess and God. Blend until the potion is thick and smooth. While you are blending it, focus on feeling more powerful and fully energized. Imagine the strength and power of the Goddess and God filling you to the brim. Makes two servings.

Blended Blessings Potion

1 ripe banana

1/2 cup orange juice

1/2 cup fat-free sweetened condensed milk

1/4 cup club soda

4 ice cubes

As you put each of the ingredients into the blender, one by one, empower them by dedicating each ingredient to a favorite divine Goddess or God. Blend all the ingredients until the potion is thick and smooth. As you do this, think about the many blessings in your life. Think about all the things you are thankful for. As you sip the potion, think of all the blessings in your life such as the people who love you. Feel the joy of these blessings empowering you. Makes two servings.

Cyber Powder Potions

Powder potions are **NOT** consumed. They are easy to make, especially with the advent of the coffee grinder. To make your cyber powder potions, first gather the ingredients together. Then hold them in your hands, and focus on putting your magickal goal *into* them. As you put each item into the grinder, dedicate it to a helpful Goddess and God. As you grind each ingredient, focus on your magickal goal. When you mix the powders together, run the powder slowly through your fingers, and focus your awareness on the magickal qualities you are imparting into the powder.

When the powder is complete, sprinkle it to release its energy. As you are sprinkling it, again focus on your magickal goal. You can sprinkle magick powder potions in a clockwise circle around you, beginning and ending in the North or East, or you can sprinkle the powder in magickal and sacred geometry shapes, for example a star or elemental cross. Try this powder potion to reduce your stress:

De-Stress Powder Potion

3 pinches of dried chamomile flowers
1 pinch of dried parsley
3 pinches of dried lavender flowers
1 pinch of dried sage

Grind all of the herbs into a fine powder in a coffee grinder. As you are doing this, charge the powder by focusing on your magickal intention. Put the powder in a bowl and run your finger through it, charging it more and more with your magickal goal. When you are done charging the potion, sprinkle it around your office, home, in your car, and any place you want to feel more relaxed.

Cleansing, Blessing, Charging, and Activating Focals

Even though they are non-traditional, Cyber Magick focals are equally worthy of your respect. Try these four methods for cleansing, blessing, charging, and activating cyber-magick focals.

Cleansing them

This can be accomplished in many ways, including rinsing edible items in cool salted water and then rinsing them again in clear water; moving items through smudge smoke of sage or cedar; and visualizing sparkling white or cobalt-blue light filling and removing any traces of negativity in the item. Thoroughly cleaning your kitchen appliances, and then wiping their surfaces with lemon or sage water is yet another way to purify them.

Blessing them

Blessing is something that can be done in many personal ways. Some Cyber Witches put their hands over the item (palm down) and merge with a favorite Goddess or God to bless it. You can also merge with the Elemental energies the item symbolizes and say a simple blessing such as, "Bless this Cyber Magick component." A simple techno-tool blessing is:

> Blessings on this fine machine,
>
> May its components all be clean.
>
> Let it keep working, without whines
>
> My cyber helpmate, throughout time.
>
> By the cyber powers that be
>
> As I will, blessed be!

Charging them

With concentration and merging, you can easily charge your components with magickal power. Charging something is akin to plugging it into the electrical current of the universe. One way to charge focals is to imagine the power of the Goddess and God pouring into the object. Move the divine energy into the item by breathing in deeply and then holding your breath for a few seconds as you focus on moving energy into the item. Then sharply exhale through your nose, not your mouth. Do this three times, and for better results, nine times. Your pulsed breath and focused intention are the carrier waves that move the energy into the item and charge it.

One way to charge your techno-tools is to put your hands on each item, and say,

> I charge this (what the tool is called) by the Ancient Ones,
>
> By the divine powers of the Goddess and God,
>
> By the powers of the sun, moon, planets, and stars
>
> By the powers of Earth, Air, Fire, and Water, and Spirit
>
> May I attain all that I desire through this tool.
>
> Great Cyber Spirits, charge it with your power!
>
> Blessed be! So shall it be!

You can also charge your techno-tools by naming them. That's right, as with the herbs, flowers, tress, plants, and stones, you can also think up names for your techno-tools. For example, "Lumina" may be your desk lamp's name, or "Rosie" your red car's name. Naming something gives it more power. Match the name to the item. To charge the tool using its power name, place your hands on the item, palms down, and say,

> With this name *(say the tool's personal name)*,
>
> I charge this cyber tool
>
> By Spirit, Earth, Air, Fire, and sea
>
> By the Great Cyber Powers that be
>
> Blessed be! So be it!

Activating them

Whisper a phrase to your cyber tools three times to activate their magickal energy, and then once more to turn them off. For example when you turn on your TV, whisper,

> Turn on your cyber charm,
>
> Protect me from any harm.

Or

> Switch on and thrive,
>
> Breathe the Elements alive.

When you turn it off, whisper,

> Turn off your cyber power,
>
> Save it for another hour.

Or

> Switch off and power down,
>
> Sleep quietly, without a sound.

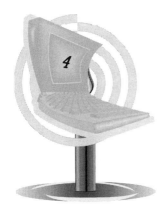

Cyber Wheel
of the Year

In mundania and the mundane world, the Wheel of Time (and life) is ever-moving. Rather than let this movement roll by without notice, it's important for Cyber Witches to keep in touch with global and universal rhythms. This sounds all well and good, except when you're constantly hooked up to technology that tends to distract you from that cadence. So how does the Techno-Pagan tune into the Wheel in a way that reflects the Cyber Path? Here are basic descriptions of the Sabbats and Esbats, together with some suggestions for keeping your hands on the Wheel of the Year.

Cyber Witch Sabbats

Most Witches celebrate the eight solar Sabbats that mark the annual cycle of the seasons. These eight Sabbats form the Wheel of the Year as they follow the path of the sun through the seasons. This "Wheel" reminds us of the never-ending, ever-beginning cycle of birth, life, death, and rebirth.

It reminds us that time is circular, not linear. The eve just before a Sabbat is the most powerful time to cast spells because the cosmic energy is at its highest.

Here is a listing of the Sabbats, their approximate dates, alternate astrological degrees, and Cyber Magick energies. Timing your spellcrafting with the Sabbats empowers your magick with the natural energy of the Elements, the seasons, and the Universe.

Winter Solstice, Yule

December 21 or 22 or 00.00 degrees   Capricorn

Cyber Magick Energies: Associated with the rebirth and blessings of the sun, this is the time to let go of the past and of reflection, building personal strength, protection, and integration. It's the shortest day and longest night of the year. Celebrate the season with loved ones, magickal cyber foods, and Yule potions. Have fun with cyber toys such as singing reindeer, musical snowmen, revolving trees that light up in different colors, and electric trains under the Yule tree.

Scents of the season include pine, cedar, bay, cinnamon, rosemary, and apple.

Imbolg, Imbolc, Bridget's Fire, Oimelc, Candlemas

February 2 or 15.00 degrees   Aquarius

Cyber Magick Energies: Associated with the sacred Fire and the flame of inspiration, which can be used to rekindle your magick, this is the time to do cyber spells for fertility, Spring cleaning, new beginnings, births, and for updating your computer files. Plant seeds, download new software, and start new files. Use this day to think about what you really want to create in your life. At dusk, light a lamp or flashlight or turn on your car headlights to welcome the sun's rebirth. Bless the light, by dedicating it to the Celtic fire Goddess Bridget by chanting,

> Bridget, Bridget, Bridget
>
> Brightest flame
>
> Bridget, Bridget, Bridget
>
> Sacred Name.

Spring Equinox, Hertha's Day, Ostara, Oestara, Eostar

March 21 or 22 or 00.00 degrees   Aries

Cyber Magick Energies: A time of balance when day and night are equal. Days become warmer, fruit trees bloom, and Nature grows stronger. Tend gardens, plant seeds and ideas, combine the Elements, do fertility spells, and overcome negative habits and obstacles. It's the perfect time for learning from Nature, sending virtual flowers over the e-mail, getting to know your power animal, and personal renewal.

Beltane, May Day, Bealtaine, and Walpurgisnacht

May 1 or 15.00 degrees   Taurus

Cyber Magick Energies: This is the time of youth and playfulness, of personal growth, love, sexuality, increased fertility, and romance. One of the prime Sabbats with lots of Fire energy for crafting powerful spells, especially love and prosperity spells. Search and click onto a virtual maypole or create a virtual balefire on the Internet to get into the cyber step of this Sabbat!

Summer Solstice, Midsummer, Letha, Litha

June 21 or 22 or 00.00 degrees   Cancer

Cyber Magick Energies: This is a time of absolute florescence, of honoring the ancestors and the Faeries, the time for harvesting herbs, flowers, and handfastings. Form new alliances with beings such as the Faeries, do shapeshifting, and get to know your power animal(s). It is the longest day and shortest night of the year.

Scents that match this Sabbat include lavender, rose, daisy, and carnation.

Lughnassad, Lammas

1st week of August or 15.00 degrees   Leo

Cyber Magick Energies: A time for annual harvesting your magickal goals, mastering skills, joining together, and handfastings. Plants begin to go to seed, so it is a time of gathering seeds (ideas), so you can plant them next Spring. Make bread with your bread maker or by hand and share it with those you care about.

Autumnal Equinox, Hellith's Day, Mabon

September 21 or 22 or 00.00 degrees   Libra

Cyber Magick Energies: A time of balance when day and night are equal, when you can sense Autumn in the air in the mornings. Harvest your magickal goals, take on new attitudes as well as set things right, and pay off old debts. Prepare for Winter.

Samhain, Halloween, Hallowmass, All Hallow's Eve

October 31 or 15.00 degrees   Scorpio

Cyber Magick Energies: When the veil between worlds is at its thinnest, it is prime time for doing all kinds of Cyber Moon Magick, including spellcrafting, divination, shapeshifting, getting in touch with your ancestors, honoring the dead, and Faery Magick. It marks the time of the last harvest of the year, and a time of personal reflection, feasting, and storytelling. Turn the heat up and put on a favorite video.

Cyber Witch Esbats

Most Cyber Witches coordinate their spells with the cycles of the moon called the Esbats. This adds powerful lunar energy. To find out which astrological sign and phase the moon is in, refer to an emphemerus or an astrology calendar. You can purchase one or you can find this information on the Internet.

Think about the cyber spell you are crafting when selecting the best moon phase to do it in. This depends upon your magickal goal. Avoid casting spells on eclipses of the moon. Here are some of the basic qualities of the different moon phases for your handy reference:

New Moon (the night of the new moon):

Spells for initiating new beginnings, new jobs, new relationships, new lovers, new ventures, and new ideas. The New Moon corresponds to the Maiden aspect of the Triple Goddess.

Waxing Moon: Spells for growth, divination, love, healing, planting seeds, protecting animals, making changes, creating new associations, rekindling romance, forming friendships, attracting prosperity, increasing good luck, networking, and working on creative projects. The Waxing Moon corresponds to the Maiden aspect of the Triple Goddess.

Full Moon (the night of the full moon):
Spells for love, inspiration, empowerment, creativity, Dream Magick, divination, healing, enhanced sexuality, fertility, prosperity, communication, shapeshifting, completing goals, and personal success. The full moon is the best time to do positive cyber spells as the lunar energy is at its highest. The full moon corresponds to the Mother aspect of the Triple Goddess.

Waning Moon: Spells for overcoming obstacles, protection, weight loss, ridding yourself of negative associations and situations, overcoming addictions, dissolving ties, changing bad luck, breaking curses, and getting rid of bad habits. the waning Moon corresponds to the Crone or Wise Woman aspect of the Goddess.

Dark or Black Moon (the three-and-a-half day period before the new moon):
Spells for protection. This is the time when lunar light is most dim. The Black Moon corresponds to the Crone aspect of the Triple Goddess.

Cyber Moon Magick Power

The 13 moons have magickal names. To figure out which Esbat matches which moon name, start counting the moons, beginning with the first full moon after the Winter Solstice (usually on December 21st or 22nd). For example, if a full moon rises on January 1st in a given year, it would be the first Esbat, called the Wolf Moon.

Some years have 13 full moons whereas others have 13 new moons. This means that in some years, there isn't a 13th full moon. The following table lists the Esbats, their magickal names, and their Moon Magick powers:

Esbat	Magickal Name	Moon Magick Powers
1st Esbat	Wolf Moon	Personal potential, loyalty, the family, trusting your instincts, shapeshifting, developing clairvoyance, and Dream Magick.
2nd Esbat	Storm Moon	Polarities, duality, creating intensity, purification, and getting rid of bad habits.
3rd Esbat	Chaste Moon	Purification, natural balance, and the trinities of Maiden/ Mother/Crone and Son/Father/ Wise Man.
4th Esbat	Seed Moon	Planting the seeds for attaining your magickal goals, starting projects, and using the powers of the Elements.
5th Esbat	Hare Moon	Balancing your ego, improving your physical environment, fertility, growth, and advancing toward your magickal goals.

Esbat	Magickal Name	Moon Magick Powers
6th Esbat	Dyad Moon	Bridging the divine and mundane, shapeshifting, Divine gifts, prosperity, and the sacred union between individuals.
7th Esbat	Mead Moon	Altered states of awareness, Dream Magick, Divine communication, healing, and absolute fluorescence.
8th Esbat	Wort Moon	Working with the natural cycles of things, putting ideas together, and formulating spells.
9th Esbat	Barley Moon	Increasing personal will, honing magickal skills, and attaining magickal goals.
10th Esbat	Wine Moon	Healing, divination, developing psychic abilities, divine inspiration, and healing power.
11th Esbat	Blood Moon	Ancestral communion, maternity, paternity, family, fellowship, and divine oaths.
12th Esbat	Snow Moon	Focusing on the Divine within, making personal and professional changes, and freezing out negativity.
13th Esbat	Oak Moon	Rebirth, shapeshifting, metamorphosis, transformation, incarnation, and transmigration.

Keeping Your Hands on the Wheel

Here are some more ideas for keeping in tune with the seasons:

Send free holiday e-cards.

It's a great way to keep in touch with family, friends, and business associates and, let them know you are thinking about them. Go ahead and send some cyber light around the world today. It's easy, free, and only takes a minute or two. There is incredible power in three little words, "I love you," or just simply, "Congratulations." There is someone right now, someone you know, who would get some joy from reading those words on his or her e-mail. Take advantage of the many sites on the Internet with e-cards. Just type the words *free e-cards* into any search engine, and pick the site that looks the best. Sirona likes to surf the Pagan and Wiccan sites for e-cards. One of her favorites is at *www.triplemoon.com*. The graphics are very witchy and fun, plus you can add music, color, and personal messages and preview the e-card before you send it.

Visit cyber gardening Web sites devoted to horticulture.

It brings Nature into your cyberspace. One of Sirona's favorite gardening sites is *www.organicgardening.com*. They e-mail a free newsletter filled with gardening tips and ideas to fit the seasonal cycles of the year, plus there are several places you can click on for gardening pictures and in-depth information.

Create seasonal screen savers for your computer.

Sirona likes to change the appearance of her desktop about every four weeks to match the Esbats and Sabbats. She pulls a graphic in from the Internet or scans a picture she likes, then matches the graphic to the time of the year. She changes the invocation or blessing on the scrolling marquee to match the graphic.

Use an electronic calendar to remind you of the unfolding of the year.

Add some seasonal graphics to your calendar to bring Nature into your virtual world. There are plenty of graphics sites out there.

Check the phases of the moon on weather and gardening sites.

Do this periodically during the month to keep you in flow with the lunar cycles.

Display clocks with faces.

These signify the 12 months of the year and the 12 zodiac signs. The two hands move clockwise (sunwise), turning in harmony with Nature. Clocks come in all shapes, so select a moon-, sun-, or star-shaped clock to remind you of the Wheel of the Year and the seasonal gifts of the Goddess.

Consider fans.

They are symbols of the Goddess, from the heater fan reminding us of Winter to the ceiling fan circulating the air in your living room in the Summer and they spin around like the Wheel of the Year.

Use plug-in air fresheners.

They come in a variety of scents, so you can match the scent to the time of year. For example, at Samhain, use an apple scented plug-in.

Watch videos and movies that follow in step with yearly cycles and holidays.

This is a simple and fun way to keep in sync with the Wheel of the Year.

Listen to holiday music.

Do this at home, in your car, during work, or when you are shopping or attending concerts to help stay in tune with the seasons.

Create a virtual tree that represents the seasons to remind you of Nature's cycles.

A virtual fruit tree buds and blossoms in the spring, grows fruit, and then loses its leaves in the fall. You can use graphics on your computer, scanned pictures, a paint program, or find graphics on the Internet to create your own virtual tree.

Display a small tabletop fountain.

Fountains with the rolling ball on the top are cyber-friendly tools of the Goddess. The rotation of the ball reminds you of the Earth Mother rotating in the universe as well as the rotation of the yearly seasons.

Stay in tune with the seasons, charged up, and on the leading edge of cyber witchery.

To keep your hand on the Wheel of the year, frequently call up your Cyber Book of Shadows and do cyber rituals on the Sabbats, either solitary or with an online group. Do cyber spellcasting daily or nightly, and even join an international Pagan chat such as the Pagan International Conferences.

Cyber Spells

Roll up your sleeves and unbutton your collar. It's time to make some magick! Now that you have a good feeling for the Cyber Witch's tools of the trade, you can start applying that information in your daily magickal practices. Before launching into this proverbial cauldron filled with spells, we'd like to briefly review the basics of sound spellcraft, and how to personalize the magickal processes in the rest of this book.

7-Step Cyber Spell Formula

There are some very important factors that make or break any spell. The first is having a *personal connection* to the symbols and processes you're about to use. If you don't understand why certain items are suggested, or they simply make no sense to you, the spell won't work. If you feel ill at ease with the suggested process, that uncertainty will undermine your spell. Quite simply, when you examine a spell here or in any other book and it doesn't excite your higher senses, find one that does. Your time is better spent on magick you enjoy doing.

Next, in finding or adapting spells, you need to *understand the full scope of your purpose*, and then *find a spell* or components that match your intention. There is absolutely nothing wrong with tweaking a prefabricated spell's procedure or components. Just remember to maintain continuity and be certain you truly trust in the changes you are making.

Third, *always take the time to cleanse, charge, and bless your components* (and the space within which you're planning to work if possible). The Cyber Witch is often working with items that have been handled a lot (think of how often people pick up and put down things in department stores). This means those items have collected a lot of random energy, not all of which is going to be helpful. Cleansing the items eliminates that unwanted energy.

Once you have a spiritually "clean" item, it makes sense to follow with charging (basically filling the battery). Many Witches place their components in sunlight (active, conscious energies) or moonlight (receptive, intuitive energies) or visualize the items being filled with brightly colored light to accomplish this part of the process. Whatever you choose, again just make sure it mirrors your goal. For example, charge a component by moonlight if you're using it in a psychic-enhancing spell (but you may also want to add a little sunlight to keep one foot grounded in reality).

Then there is the blessing. A blessing is a prayer. It's a type of consecration with a specific goal. When we bless pets, children, and homes, we're expressing our wishes to the Divine that those people and places are safe, happy, and generally free from temporal concerns. We also bless items as a way of imprinting them with sacred energies suited to their task(s), in this case our components.

Historically speaking blessings took two popular forms, a prayer or the laying on of hands (to symbolize the transfer of energy). Both of these approaches are perfectly suited to Cyber Witchery. Use the one you are most comfortable with.

Fourth, once everything's ready there's still the personal equation to consider. *Are you ready?* Take the time to settle your body, mind, and spirit before beginning the spell. This momentary pause also gives you an important opportunity to ponder your motivations for the magick one last time, making sure your heart, mind, and spirit are in the right place for the task at hand.

Fifth, *cast the spell*. Shape your thoughts, then transmit that willful purpose through your components, words, and actions. As you do this keep your eye on the mark. Release the energy, and then direct and guide it as far as possible (assigning it to the person, place, situation, or thing to which you want the energy to attach itself).

Sixth, after you release the spell, *ground yourself*. Sit down, take a walk, or take a warm bath. Take a few cleansing breaths and relax. Ask yourself how you feel, and how the spell felt. This is a good opportunity to find your personal gage for whether or not a spell went smoothly.

Last, but most importantly, *follow up on what you've done with both word and deed*. Cyber Witches know they have to give the universe ample opportunity to answer our magick with manifestation (it's part of being a co-creator and remaining responsive and responsible). With all due respect, if you're not willing to put in the effort, don't do the magick (you will be disappointed).

So there it is. If you follow this seven-step guideline, we think you'll find your cyber-spell efforts far more fulfilling and successful.

Spells

Abundance

The scope of the word *abundance* is often overlooked. When we talk of abundance, we often think cold-hard cash, but true abundance is certainly not limited to our pocketbooks. Rather, in the context of this book (and these spells) abundance includes things such as having bounteous love and friendship, a profusion of luck in the garden (or supermarket), and so forth.

Dust Bunny Bounty

The one thing that always multiplies in the house is the dust bunny. You never really get rid of them! Why not use that positive symbolism the next time you clean? Gather all the dust bunnies together and incant over them,

> Even as these increase,
>
> May my luck never cease.
>
> And as through the winds they bounce and dance,
>
> Bring to me abundance.

Release the dustpan filled with the dust bunnies to the winds (either out the back door or a window).

Plentiful Pomegranate

Because of the number of seeds in a pomegranate, they are the perfect symbol of abundance. Sprinkle a few seeds in your window boxes or garden so plants grow richly. Eat a few and internalize the energy of abundance, then dry a few and keep them as cyber components for any spell that needs abundant energy. For example, if your computer keeps drawing too much power, put a few of these in a film canister and keep it next to the surge protector. Charge them by saying,

> By the power of pomegranate seeds,
>
> Protect and empower this energy feed!

Awareness

If we look in a dictionary, it's interesting to see that this word means watchful, vigilant, cautious, and apprised. Spiritually speaking, awareness is a unique quality that often boils down to staying awake and keeping our magickal senses tightly tuned. When you're working with the unique energies created by Cyber Witchery, this is very important. In fact, it's doubly so, because we're making every effort to move magick into the future with our transforming realities in mind.

Alarm Awareness

Most watches, palm pilots, and even some cell phones alert us to something specific (direct our awareness). You can use this symbolism and the sound of the alarm as a helpmate in awareness magick. In this case I suggest saturating the alarm function itself with a spell. Think of a color that represents awareness and visualize that hue as light pouring into the buttons on the item you've chosen. (If you have to hit a set of function keys, make sure the alarm function is showing on the item's face.) Repeat this incantation while that function's active:

> By your sounding keep me aware,
>
> Be the sign foul or fair.
>
> Ever watchful, vigilant ward,
>
> Into this _____ my will is poured.
>
> Blessed be! So mote it be!

Caffeine Alert

Many of us drink coffee and other caffeinated beverages to wake up and refresh ourselves. This spell applies the physical effect of caffeine with our magickal will. Rather than simply drinking your next cup or glass, hold it with one hand and focus on your intention. With the other hand, stir the beverage clockwise to generate positive energy while saying,

Around, around, awareness abounds!

Repeat the incantation several times until the beverage is swirling then drink it immediately to internalize the magick.

Banishing

Banishing has two different aspects. The first is driving a specific type of energy away from you, by force if need be.

Note: When I say "force" here it means force of will in magickal terms.

The second aspect of banishing is a declaration. This type of banishing certainly makes sense. For example, when we correct children for bad behavior, we announce the wrongness to them with a forceful voice (in the hopes of banishing that behavior). Applying this principal magickally is simple. It equates to a verbalized spell (a charm) that announces your resolve to the four winds.

Garbage-Disposal Banishing

The use of poppets is very old. For this spell, use a small piece of potato. Shape it to represent the negative person or situation that requires banishing. Focus intently on that individual or situation and all the specifics of it. Hold the finished symbol in your power hand (right hand if you are right-handed). Say,

No longer harm, and keep away.

As this potato disappears,

So too keep _____ at bay.

Fill in the blank with the name of who or what you are banishing and then put the symbolic potato in the disposal. turn on your magick!

Flush It

The toilet is one of my favorite techno-tools for getting rid of the proverbial crap in my life. The spell is quite simple. On a sturdy (two-ply) piece of toilet paper write down whatever you wish to banish. Visualize that situation or energy in as much detail as possible. Then toss it in the toilet and flush it away. Turn away and don't look back (to look back accepts the energy back into your life). The water dissolves the paper and washes away the negative energy. Note: this method is not recommended for those with septic systems.

Cleansing

The idea behind cleansing anything is to rid the item, area, or person of unwanted energies. Remember that not all such energies are "bad" or "negative"per se, but different from those that you hope to produce by your magick. Some common household items that come to mind immediately as perfect components for spiritual clean-up duty include brooms (of course), mops, vacuum cleaners, hand soap, scouring pads, and kitchen brushes. Here are some spells to get you started cleaning things up.

Auric Purification

The next time you go shopping look for a soap that has a cleansing scent. There are lots of stores that stock specialty soaps. Aromas to consider include lemon, lavender, pine, sandalwood, and sage. Then, before you enact a spell or ritual, take a hot shower using the soap. Move it over your body in a counterclockwise manner saying,

> Away, away, negativity away.

Now reverse the process and move clockwise saying,

> To me, to me, bring blessings to me!

As you step out of the shower don't look back until all the excess water has disappeared, neatly taking your unwanted energy with it down the drain!

Suck It Up

It doesn't matter where your sacred space is located, there are going to be times when you want to do spiritual maintenance. One of the easiest ways to accomplish this is by sprinkling the rugs and furniture in that space with baking soda or a fabric freshener saying,

> Absorb what I no longer need,
>
> By my will this spell is freed.

Let the soda or fabric freshener sit for a few minutes, then use your upright or hand vacuum to gather up that energy (which then gets disposed with the vacuum bag). Note: You can make a serviceable fabric freshener out of baking soda and herbs that represent what you most need, such as powdered rose for love or lavender for peace among roommates.

Comeliness

All of us like to feel attractive, and all of us certainly have those proverbial bad hair days! When those days come, having a couple of comeliness spells and talismans tucked away definitely comes in handy. We mention talismans because the beauty industry has provided us with some potentially great portable items to use in our spellcraft. Examples include lip balm, foundation powder, skin lotion, compact mirrors, and tweezers.

Lip-Balm Beauty

If you can find a lip balm that includes aloe, all the better, because it has been used in beauty spells historically. Wait until the night of a full moon and stand beneath its beams (if you can't wait, do this by candlelight). Now repeat this incantation three times,

> Into my aura, come gentle light,
>
> Make of me a beautiful/handsome sight.
>
> When to my lips this balm apply,
>
> Help me catch appreciative eyes!
>
> As I will, so shall it be!

Put this balm on just before going to a nightclub, party, class, or any place you're likely to feel like you could use a boost of self-confidence.

Compact Comeliness

We're going to have a little fun playing with the lines from Sleeping Beauty for this spell. First, find a small mirror suited to carrying with you in a wallet, purse, belt pouch, or briefcase. You'll also need some heather- (or flower-) scented soap or oil (heather was used in beauty spells in Scotland). Second, consider a symbol that you equate with attractiveness. If you find your attention drawn to a person's neck, use the symbol of two slightly curved parallel lines (the shape of a neck). If you find your attention drawn to a person's eyes, use the symbol of two eye shapes with center dots. On the back of the mirror, draw this emblem using the soap or oil while saying,

> Mirror, Mirror in my hand,
>
> Remove all energies dull and bland.
>
> Mirror, Mirror in this hour,
>
> Bring to me guising power.
>
> Mirror, Mirror the magick's free,
>
> Attractiveness without and within—it's ME!

Carry the mirror with you.

Communication

It's the information age, so the Cyber Witch will most likely get this one right! E-mail in particular is known to cause all kinds of trouble because the person on the other end can't see your face or hear verbal inflections (which is why emoticons were invented!). Thus these cyber spells are aimed at all forms of communication: virtual, verbal, written, and even body language!

Keyboard Communication

Use this spell when you're concerned that your Internet missives might be misunderstood by the intended party. Take a bay leaf and write the name of the person to whom the e-mail is going. Wrap this in a white napkin and put it under your keyboard. This keeps "bugs" out of your letter and also protects your words. Type the letter with the bay leaf secured under the keyboard the whole time. When at last you click the "Send" key, remove the bay leaf and burn it to release your true intentions to that person and send the missives on the wind.

Telephone Tag

There is nothing more frustrating than spending days in telephone tag. So why not try to avoid this problem by making a special charm for your telephone? Take a small snippet of yellow cloth (the color of communication and creativity) and wrap an amethyst and a small piece of hazelwood therein. Amethyst encourages rectification/resolution; hazel was traditionally used in divination so you can figure out the best time to call! Charge this bundle by the light of a waxing moon (growing toward your goal) or in an Easterly wind that bears the energy of communication. Then leave it near your phone. By the way, this works if you have a pouch for your cell phone, too!

Sweet Words

Our "out loud" voice often gets the best of us in trouble. Words come tumbling out of our lips and we immediately regret them. This spell is designed to avoid that situation. For it you'll need a container of breath mints (any type). Set them in the light of a noonday sun to encourage forethought and wisdom, and empower them saying,

> By my will and the power of the sun,
>
> Wisdom's evoked, the spell's begun.
>
> Through vital breath these sweet mints convey,
>
> Honorable words all the day!

Enjoy one just before going into situations where you might be tempted to say things you might regret later.

Courage

It takes a healthy dose of backbone to be a Cyber Witch or any type of Witch, for that matter. Even with the Harry

Potter craze and all the progress we've made, the public still doesn't completely understand what we do or why we do it. Facing this on a daily basis can really test a person's mettle. Spells for courage are designed to fill in during those moments when weary uncertainty and natural fears threaten to upset the daily apple cart.

Courageous Clothing

Think of courage as a mantle that we wrap around ourselves. With that in mind, find an item of red clothing (if it's an undergarment or socks, all the better, these "support" everything else). Toss the item in the dryer. Put some thyme and/or borage (both known for brave energies) in an old knee-high nylon stocking or wrap some of these herbs up in a piece of cheesecloth, and then toss this into the dryer, too. The heat of the dryer releases both the aroma and energies of the herb into that piece of clothing, which you then put on to likewise "put on" the magick. By the way, this spell can be altered for any goal, using any item of clothing. Just make sure that the item's color and the herbs match your intention.

Firm Feet

Use this spell when you're having trouble standing your ground. Take ¼ cup of baking soda, ½ tsp. black tea leaves, ½ tsp. of thyme, ½ tsp. of mint (mental clarity), and ½ tsp. of bay (strength), and mix them together. As you're stirring add an incantation such as,

> Steady and sure,
>
> I'll stand my ground,
>
> As my magick wraps around.

Sure and bold,

I'll speak my case,

This powder all fears now, ERASE!

Sprinkle this liberally into your shoes before going out.

Devotion

Ah, that sublime word *commitment* that seems to leave the bravest of souls quivering. Why? Because commitment and devotion open us up. They're sunlight to the flower of our heart and soul. When you're open you're, unfortunately, also vulnerable to being hurt, disillusioned, and downright used. With this in mind, these spells are designed to support your sense of earnestness by balancing that go-get-'em attitude with wisdom.

Tie It Up

When I think of devotion, I think of those things to which we willingly bind ourselves such as spouses, children, and pets. So, for this spell you'll need a tie or scarf that represents the area in your life that you'd like to have a little more faith in. Hold the tie or scarf in one hand and begin knotting it with the other. As you tie the knots, recite this incantation:

With the knot of one the spell's begun.

With the knot of two, my focus is true.

With the knot of three, devotion blossom in me.

With the knot of four, zeal into me pour.

With the knot of five, my spell comes alive.

As I will, so mote it be.

Untie one knot the next time you need this energy released into your life. Never, however, untie the *first* knot. When you get to that point, recharge the tie/scarf.

Duct-Tape Tenacity

If you want to "stick to it" with regard to a particular project, person, or whatever, what better to fit that bill than the ever-amazing duct tape. (By the way, duct tape is known jokingly as the "force" in many Neo-Pagan circles because it's grayish/black on one side, white on the other, and holds everything together.) For this spell you'll need a fair length of duct tape (about 3'), something that represents you, and something that represents the person or project. These items should either be disposable or ones that won't be damaged by the tape. Gather them, wrapping the duct tape around everything, saying,

> Focus my intent, my heart, my hands,
>
> Let me see this through from start to end.

When you no longer need the stick-to-itiveness of this spell, remove the tape and separate the items.

Divination

Divination is all about looking at future patterns. Sometimes these patterns can't be changed, even when you try change the outcome. This is not to say the future is written in stone or that it can't be changed. Movement through time produces certain patterns and these patterns have a tendency to move in somewhat predictable ways. Magick is the practice of noticing and influencing these patterns through expectation, desire, and merging. You can use cyber divination to do just that!

Divine Surfing

A variety of interactive oracles including tarot, runes, I Ching, numerology, fortune cookies, word oracle, and astrology are readily available on the Internet. Choose from sites such as iching.com (an excellent I Ching site), *facade.com*, *tarotmagic.com* (hundreds of decks to choose from), *thenewage.com*, or *dreampower.com*, to name just a few. Click on and have fun divining your future. If you don't like a particularly reading, just keep clicking on until you do!

TV Scrying

This spell uses a blank TV screen as a scrying mirror. Do this spell at night on the full moon. First, clear the screen out by visualizing pure white light pulsing through it. If your screen automatically switches to cobalt blue when you turn off your VCR, then use the cobalt blue screen to clean any unwanted negativity out of the screen. When you are ready, make sure the TV and the lights are off. It's easier to scry in a dark room.

Sit in front of the TV and light two candles. Match the candle color to your scrying goal. Put the candles in front (on both sides) of the screen. Candlelight helps you to see images on the screen. If you like, you can use a two penlights for this purpose. Close your eyes for a few minutes and relax, using deep breathing. Just let go of all your thoughts and worries for a few minutes. When you open your eyes, put your hands on the screen to make the connection with your techno-scrying mirror. Gaze at the screen and think about the information that you are seeking. Gaze into the screen, looking at the patterns of light and shadow as they move around the screen. Do this for at least 15 minutes. Next, move your mind beyond the screen and merge with the light patterns. The images trigger impressions that relate to your reason for scrying. After you are finished, note the images and messages you received. Clean your TV screen out with white light again (or use the cobalt blue screen). You can either allow the candles to safely burn out, or snuff them and use them again for cyber scrying.

Dreams

What's in a dream? Many magickally minded people feel that dreams bear messages from spirit guides and the Divine. Some of these dreams predict the future or explain the past. But how do we go about inspiring those spiritually oriented dreams? These spells create the right energies to open that doorway.

Cyber Dream Catcher

Native American-styled dream catchers have become popular decorative items, but what about something suited to the Cyber Witch? Gather together a metallic hoop, a speaker wire, a memory chip from the computer (used), and a magnet any time during a waxing to full moon. This timing accentuates the intuitive and spiritual nature. The magnet attracts spiritual dreams, and the memory chip helps you recall them! Use the speaker wire to make a web inside the hoop attaching the magnet and memory chip wherever you'd like them to go. Each time you knot the wire to secure it, add a specific intention such as,

> Here I bind nightmares to keep them away.

Or

> Here I welcome Spirit to speak to me in my dreams.

Hang this near your bed.

Dreamtime Tea

For this tea I recommend a blend of organic marigold and organic rose petals (1/4 cup each covered in water). Both these flowers are respected for their ability to manifest dreams. Put the flowers and water in the microwave oven for 45 seconds. If it rotates clockwise, all the better as that helps build positive energy. Remove from the microwave and let the tea steep. As it does, hold your hands down over the liquid and invoke your favorite Goddess or God to bless your dreams. In particular, invite her or him into your dreams. (Note: Sometimes playing soft music or burning jasmine incense helps the results of this spell.) Consume the tea right before you go to bed. Remember that not *all* roses are safe for consumption.

Employment

Cyber Witches come from all walks of life. Some are wealthy and self-employed, but most are just trying to make enough money to pay their bills from month to month the way most folks are. Consequently, having a job that's not only enjoyable but that meets our financial needs is important. Emotionally, people in good jobs have more positive energy to direct into magick. When you're job hunting, seeking promotions, or even working on a lateral move that's more fulfilling, try these spells to support those efforts:

Want-Ad Window Shopping

Some of the best places to window shop for a new job are your local and online want ads. In either, you can get a better feel for what's out there in your field (or realm of experience) that you'd really enjoy. Put together 13 of these (the number of full moons in a year). If you're gathering your lists from the Net, print them out then cut out the ones you want. Rubber band these inside your business card or resume and leave it on your altar, voicing your wishes. At least once a week go back to the altar, light a candle, and repeat your wishes. Then check the want ads. Send out resumes to those that have similar appeal as those on your altar. Continue this for 12 weeks and watch doors open for you.

Pen Persistency

Inevitably when you're out job hunting you'll have to fill out applications. The market is filled with all kinds of high-tech pens just begging for the Cyber Witch's attention, so why not get one and energize if for employment success? Select a blue one (a professional color) and a tip-size that shows off your best handwriting (neatness counts!). Hold the pen in your hands before you begin writing and mentally say,

> The job I want is in my sights,
>
> I take this pen with which to write.
>
> Employers notice this magick blue,
>
> And call me for an interview!

Now fill out those forms confidently.

In the Right Place at the Right Time

For a successful job interview, use your digital clock. On the morning of the job interview, take a few moments before you get ready, and first set your digital clock for 8:00 (eight is the number of business and prosperity). Say aloud three times,

> Sacred eight of prosperity
>
> Bring success now to me.
>
> So be it! Blessed be!

Close your eyes, take a few deep breaths, and then imagine the interview being successful. See and sense yourself answering the questions just right, having a very positive interview experience, and getting the job. Then get ready for your interview, taking special care with your appearance. Just before going through the door into the interview, say to yourself,

Success is coming to me.

Blessed be!

Energy

Cyber Witches and Pagans usually have pretty full plates in life. They juggle homes, one or more jobs, children, hobbies, and their spirituality. At times they can get completely exhausted. Energy spells are designed to temporarily help us over those bumps or to boost the power in spells and rituals. We do not recommend using them as a substitute for a good night's sleep. Plenty of sound sleep charges your body, mind, and spirit, but when you need a personal power, and shut-eye time isn't a possibility, try these spells.

Charge It Up

This spell utilizes any small battery as its focus (AA and AAA are good choices). This should be a new or barely used battery (most of its power remaining still intact). Go outside with the battery at noon. This is the hour of high power, and sunlight represents a formidable source of energy. Hold the battery in the palm of both hands, saying,

Light and power of the sun,

Hear me in this hour.

By my will this spell's begun,

Saturate this charm with power!

Repeat the incantation eight times (the number representing power and the growth-oriented energies of a double-Earth
Element). Carry the battery in a handy location, touching it,
and repeating the incantation once (the sun's number) to release a little boost when you need it.

Hosing Up Power

Just as you water your plants with a hose to nourish and
refresh them, you can also use the hose to energize yourself.
At noon on a hot Summer's day, go outside and turn on the
water hose. Water your flowers, lawn, trees, and so forth, and
then put your thumb over the hose to squirt the water around.
As you do this turn the hose upward, over your head and
shower yourself with the water. Each time you do this, say,

> Sweet droplets of energy,
>
> From head to toe, restore me
>
> As I will, so be it!

As the water drops rain down on your, imagine they are
wet refreshing gifts from the Goddess.

Castles in Your Mind

Fashioned from your imagination, your mind castle is a
personal power place where you can recharge your batteries.
Sirona's mind castle looks similar to a traditional Scottish
castle, with magnificent water gardens, tall sweet-smelling ce-
dars, and large spires of clear quartz crystal rising up behind
it. When the sun hits the crystals, it's dazzling! To get in touch
with your own mind castle, you will need something with a
quartz crystal in it, such as a watch. Put on some soft music,
lay down or sit back, and hold the watch in your receptive

hand (left if you are right-handed). Then close your eyes and breathe deeply. Calm your mind and let go of any tension as you exhale. Imagine a magickal castle with the sun shining down upon it in your mind's eye. Create your castle exactly the way you want it. Name it, to personalize its power even more. Begin to visualize walking into your mind castle. Imagine the sun shining brightly on the castle walls as you enter. As you explore the interior of the castle, select a sunny room, with lots of windows. As you stand in this sunny room, feel the warmth of the sun coming through the window. Now imagine a thick golden cord of sun energy connecting you to your castle, and, as you take a deep breath, sense all of the magickal energy of your castle flowing through the cord into you. Take several deep breaths and fill yourself with golden energy. Then imagine a sphere of bright golden light radiating from your heart. Imagine breathing this golden light outward into the skies with your every exhale. Use rhythmic breathing to amplify your shining gold radiance, feeling it growing stronger with each breath you take. Imagine yourself becoming a bright sun. Drink in the solar energy, its power, and its vitality through the gold cord. Visualize your energy field becoming so bright that you light up the entire castle. Breathe this energy into your being, and repeat three times,

I am filled with blessed light.

I am the sun shining bright.

Stay in your castle as long as you want, exploring and enjoying its magickal power. You can repeat this visualization any time you need a burst of energy. When you are in a time pinch, just touch the face of your watch and say the blessing three times to yourself to immediately feel more energized.

Note: You can also create a virtual castle by saving a castle graphic from the Internet or by scanning a picture of a favorite castle.

Forgiveness

Humans like to be right, and we often hold on tightly to those things we should leave in the past for everyone's betterment. Forgiveness spells help us to do that and to begin the healing process.

Chill Out

Before forgiveness happens, anger has to wane. To help with this, make a poppet of each person from whom the anger is originating (including yourself). Be very clear of your intention here (to simply alleviate the anger, *not* harm anyone). At this juncture you can put the poppet in one of two places: in front of the air conditioning unit or in the freezer. The air conditioner provides a gentler cooling, where the freezer is better suited when tempers are really out of control and you really want to freeze the problem out of your life. Leave the poppet in place until the door for forgiveness and healing opens to you. Then bury it.

Bandage the Boo-Boo

In ancient times people would apply salve to a knife that wounded them in the belief that this "forgiveness" toward the blade would help the healing process along. Bringing that idea into a modern construct, find a picture of someone whose hurt you and toward whom you're having trouble extending forgiveness. Also get an adhesive bandage. Sit down in front of the picture and say everything you wish you could say to that person. Don't hold back—just let it pour out. When you finally feel empty, take the bandage and apply it to that picture and say,

I forgive you.

What is done is done.

The past behind us,

The future before.

I shall not speak of this again.

What you do with the picture at this point depends a lot on whether you will ever see that individual again. If you will, keep the image safe somewhere to continue generating that healing energy. If not, burn the picture so as to not dredge up any remnant negative memories.

Friendship

Good friends are among life's most precious things, and the Cyber Witch certainly wishes to build solid friendships and strong networking ties in his or her community. Friendship spells can help with that as long as we remember that friendship, similar to love, should not be manipulated or coerced.

Web of Well-Wishing

For this spell you'll need an 8 1/2 × 11 piece of paper on which you've drawn something that resembles a spider web. In the center of the web, write your name or put a picture of yourself. Then on each strand of the web write the e-mail addresses of the people you value as friends. If you can do this with pink ink, all the better (pink is a friendship color, implying a type of gentle love and understanding). Otherwise use blue ink to extend peace and happiness to each. When you're done, place your hands palm down over the paper and visualize it surrounded by sparkling white light, the color of protection, to keep your friends safe. Store this in a safe place, preferably on or near your altar so those people benefit from all your magick.

E-Card Energy

Go to your favorite search engine and look for e-card shops (there are tons of free ones). Now, think of a person in your life with whom you'd like to build a stronger friendship. Look for an e-card that will brighten his or her day or one that expresses how you feel. When you find the perfect card, fill out all the information requested on that Web site but do not send it yet. Hold the index finger of your strong hand over the send key and recite this incantation,

> From me to you,
>
> From you to me,
>
> I open the lines
>
> Of energy.
>
> A friend to have,
>
> A friend to hold,
>
> By my will, this spell unfolds!

As you say "unfolds" hit the send option so it conveys your magick with the e-card.

Global Healing

Cyber Witches like to play, but we recognize that we can't be all play and no work, especially when it comes to protecting our planet, the Mother Earth. Technology has brought many wonders, but it's also facilitated many of the Earth's problems in terms of global ecology. While we're enacting various mundane efforts to help fix those problems, our magick can begin wrapping around the planet like a balm.

Keychain Charm

You can purchase little globekey chains. They're designed to look like the Earth from space and are really quite pretty (they seem to be available nearly anywhere that sells gift items). Get yourself one of these, a strip of white cloth, and any type of healing salve you have around the house. Put a little of the salve on the cloth (as a make-shift bandage). Wrap the cloth clockwise around the little globe, saying,

> Little Earth wrapped in balm,
>
> To protect the planet from further harm
>
> The Earth be whole, the Earth to heal,
>
> By my will, the magick's sealed.

Keep this in a safe place or on your altar.

Wallpaper Wellness

There are several places on the Internet where you can find wallpaper images of the Earth from space. Find one and load it onto your computer screen. That way whenever you have a spare moment you can focus positive energy toward the planet and have a strong visual cue to support your efforts. To this process you could add a prayer. Say,

> Earth, our Mother, sustain us.
>
> People, your children, renew and keep you.
>
> North, East, South, and West,
>
> Gods and Goddesses the world bless!

Grounding

Cyber Witches work with electricity often. Knowing how to ground is nothing less than essential (at least if we want our magickal currents to flow properly!). Beyond this very practical function, grounding spells help us build sound foundations to our spirituality and keep one foot in "terra-firma" while we're exploring the esoteric world.

Plant It!

Whether you are a city or country Witch, most Neo-Pagans like having something green and growing around their living space. For this spell you'll need some soil or a potted plant. Stand in front of the container with a small stone (or any other small item that can represent the area of your life in need of more "roots") cupped in the palm of both your hands. Name this token, whispering its purpose to it, then sow it into that soil. As you do this, say,

> Planted by my hand,
>
> Into the soil, and into the land.
>
> Foundations take root and grow,
>
> As above so below!

If you're using plain soil, add a small seedling so the token grows alongside that plant's roots (for improved symbolism).

Coffee Grounding

Save some of the grounds from the next pot of coffee you make. Their typical energetic effects have already been transferred into the water, so you now have a magickally neutral substance. Take these "grounds" outside and sprinkle them in a circle around yourself, saying,

> Grounds to the ground,
>
> Around and around,
>
> Help me keep my feet on the ground.

Health

I'm sure your mother told you "if you have your health, you have everything." However, health spells need not simply apply to the body. For example, a health spell can be cast to improve the figurative well-being of a relationship or to heal a tract of land that's holding a negative psychic imprint. Keep this in mind as you read these spells so you can adapt them to other functions.

Broth Betterment

As Kitchen Witches, we often turn to various foods and beverages as magickal components. What's truly wonderful is that technology has brought many "instant" foods into our homes that take very little time to prepare This can be important when you're feeling under the weather. This spell looks to bouillon cubes as its key ingredient. Prepare the soup or broth according to directions, but as you stir make sure to turn your spoon counterclockwise to banish sickness. Throughout this process repeat an incantation. Say,

> Wherever sickness currently dwells,
>
> Remove it now and make me well!

Drink expectantly, then go get some much-needed rest.

Comfort-Food Fitness

Everyone has something they prefer to eat when they're sick. Even if this item isn't "good" for you, emotionally it provides what we call "warm fuzzies"—that sense of pleasure despite the circumstances. For this spell you'll need your favorite comfort food. Put it in the light of the sun for a few minutes (historically sunlight was considered very healthy and something that encouraged blessings). If it's not sunny out, turn to technology and use the light from full-spectrum bulbs instead. With ice cream, just saturate if for a minute, so it won't melt on you. While the item sits in that light, focus on your intention, saying,

> Gladden my heart, bring good cheer,
>
> Laughter and health are welcome here.
>
> Where blessed sunlight saturates,
>
> All sadness and sickness must abate!

Enjoy your solar-charged comfort food!

Humor

Laughter is good soul food and it's a popular pastime among Cyber Witches. Humor also affords tremendous teaching and healing energies. So the next time you're feeling grumpy or a little blue, tickle your fancy and try out these spells:

Joke URL Jollies

There are a lot of great Web sites dedicated to jokes (and specific types of jokes at that). When you find yourself down in the dumps, take a few moments to go surfing. Just before you try finding a site, hold your hands toward your computer, visualizing a pink-white light pouring out from them towards it (so you'll be "in the pink"). Try an incantation such as:

> Humor be quick,
>
> Humor be kind,
>
> Banish the blues
>
> And my sorrowful mind.

Now go and see what gives you a good giggle. Internalize that happiness.

Feather Fancy

Feathers are pretty easy to come by in nearly any size, shape, and color you wish. For this spell try to locate one that appeals to you visually and is a color that reminds you of happiness (such as yellow or sky blue). Next, stand up and move the feather through your aura from close to your skin outward to brush away any negativity. You can use the same incantation from the previous humor spell, or perhaps something such as this:

> I'm not being fickle,
>
> Magick, my fancy to tickle.
>
> Carry negativity away
>
> Bring good humor today!

Inspiration/Innovation

Perhaps two of the greatest tools of the Cyber Witch, inspiration and innovation are essential to our practice. When magick and spirituality stagnate, they die. Because Cyber Magick tries to keep up with technological advances, we've no small task in our hands. The Cyber Witch armed with a creative eye, however, can do just about anything with whatever the world dishes out.

Winds of Wonder

Depending on the season, go to an Easterly facing window, or place an electrical fan in the Eastern Quarter of your sacred space (turned off). Stand before the window or fan and close your eyes for a minute. Let go of the stress and burdens that often hinder creative flow. Now begin to chant very softly,

> With winds that blow, creativity flows.

Keep repeating this phrase until your voice naturally begins to get louder. As you feel the energy reaching a peak, open your eyes, open the window, and turn on the fan to receive the winds of inspiration. Enjoy them for a few minutes, make some quick notes of your creative ideas, then take that energy with you into your tasks for the day.

Tenacious Tea

Inspiration is, in part, related to perspiration! If you give up too soon, that flash of insight could be lost forever. So when you feel as if the creative flow is blocked and you're ready to give up, try this tea. Take regular black tea (for power) and put two allspice berries in it (for the partnership between you and your inventive higher self). Let this steep in hot water until it's heady. Add a spoonful of honey, stirring clockwise, saying,

> Honey of the muse, release in me,
>
> My sense of creativity!
>
> By my will this spell is spun,
>
> I hereby claim renewed determination!

Drink the full cup to internalize the magick. By the way, if you need this energy to manifest more quickly, heat the tea in your microwave before stirring in the honey.

Joy

Next to health, happiness is a key ingredient to a fulfilling personal and spiritual life. The saying "if it doesn't make you happy, why do it?" is one of the Cyber Witch mottos! Thus, these spells are designed to surround the practitioner with joy-attracting vibrations so that every day has at least one moment of pure, unbridled bliss.

Bubble Bliss

For this spell you'll need a small bottle of children's bubbles and a blower along with a little mint extract (an aroma that supports happiness). Put just one or two drops of the mint into the liquid bubbles. Dip in the blower and, as you create bubbles, exhale your negativity into them. Then take your hand and neatly break the bubbles in the air to wipe away those bad vibes, and release the aroma of the mint to surround you with joy. You can use a fan to blow the bubbles around to intensify the experience. Balloons work for this spell, too. Just dab the mint extract on the exterior of the balloon. You need to be certain to dispose of the balloons properly so no wandering child or animal accidentally chokes on them.

Chocolate Congeniality

There's a chocoholic that lives inside a lot of people just waiting to have a good excuse to binge. And if moments of depression aren't a good reason, what is? For those who may have chocolate allergies, carob may be substituted. For this spell you'll need a bar of your favorite type of chocolate and a small, sweet orange. Peel the orange, visualizing yourself peeling away the dark clouds hovering over your spirit. Afterward, melt the chocolate in a double boiler and let it cool just a bit. Dip each slice of the orange into the chocolate, cool, then bless it saying,

> Sealed herein with a chocolate kiss,
>
> I gift myself with a bit of bliss!

Eat a couple slices and share the rest with someone else you know who has been feeling a little blue. Happiness is a dish best shared!

Justice [Legal Matters]

Justice has two faces. The first is the face we see[:-)], or don't see [:-( ], in our legal system. The second is the sense of justice we often seek on a personal level, and one that normal legal channels cannot touch [;-)]. In both cases, however, fairness and equity are at the root of the need. When you face issues on either front, these spells should help open the way for renewed balance.

Karmic Kickback

There are times in everyone's life when we'd like karma to work for us. In this case, if you need back some "good stuff" to help you through a legal situation, try this spell. (Note: Please be careful here. If there's a real reason that you're in trouble legally, this spell will worsen the situation rather than help it.) Take a small, hand-held mirror and a picture of yourself. Glue the picture face down, saying,

> That which I've released, return now to me,
>
> By the law of three by three, so mote it be!

If you have done only good and ended up caught in a bad situation, this spell helps return your goodness by way of smoothing things out.

An alternative application for this spell is when you believe someone has harmed you and wish to return his or her energy to him or her. In this case you put that person's picture or name face down on the mirror and say,

> That which _____ *(name of person)* _____
> released, return now to _____ *(her or him)* _____ .
>
> By the law of three by three, so mote it be!

This process forces that person to see her or himself in truthfulness, and returns whatever he or she sends out toward you directly back to him or her. What's nice about this spell is if you're wrong and that person is doing no ill, *nothing* happens!

Balance the Scales

Take an item that represents the situation in which justice is needed (if you have legal documents, that's a good choice). Now, take your bathroom scale and put it on a table before you with the item(s) on top. Slowly begin adjusting the scale back to zero while you say,

> Justice be not blind,
>
> The balance restore,
>
> The truth to find,
>
> Lies shall trouble me no more!

If you leave the scale and the item(s) like that until after the situation is resolved, it further supports your magick.

Knowledge/Learning

Cyber Witches tend to have ravenously hungry minds. We are forever questing to learn or try something new, especially something that might help our Craft. Nonetheless, there come moments when our minds reach critical mass with input or when we simply find ourselves unable to focus. In those moments, look to these spells to strengthen your conscious mind and renew your mental clarity.

The Eyes Have It!

We know that the eyes are most definitely associated with learning as we take in so much information from the world through them. For this spell you'll need a pair of play eye glasses (such as those in toy stores or those specifically for fashion). Take the glasses out into the light of a nice, sunny day (the sunlight illuminates your conscious mind). Dab them with a bit of rosemary oil (to improve your memory). If you can't locate this oil, lilac and honeysuckle are two alternatives that support mental functions. Keep these near where you do most of your studying, and when you find your thoughts wandering, put them on and say,

> Information to know, focus bestow!
>
> Wandering thoughts turn, it's time to learn!

Leave them in place for a few minutes to get in focus, begin releasing the magick, and get back to work!

The Pen Is Mightier

If we're not typing or recording, we're writing as we study. Take advantage of this by energizing your pen for mental accuracy. First, find the type of pen with which you really like writing. Look for a color that represents learning. A gold or yellow pen is traditional. Each time you us the pen to help keep you on track, recite this incantation:

> As I take this pen in hand to write,
>
> Keep my needs and goals in sight.
>
> It is for knowledge that I yearn,
>
> This material I will learn.

Love

Ah love, that all elusive, and often confusing, emotion. Love has so many facets. There's love for an art form, love of a spiritual path, love toward a child, love toward a pet companion, and romantic love (just to name a few). Unfortunately, a lot of people only use love spells for the last purpose, to try and snare a mate. Although its natural to want to be desired, it can be frustration to always wonder if someone loves you for *you*, or because of a spell. So think carefully about how you extend these love spells. We've written them in such a way as to try not to manipulate other's free will and strongly suggest that any revisions you make follow that protocol.

Say it With Flowers

This is a beautiful spell that opens the way for love without manipulation. It also encourages self-love. For this spell, you'll need about c cup corn starch and some dried rose petals. Put these in a coffee grinder or food processor and blend them together into a fine powder. Do this on a Friday (the day of the week associated with love) or, better yet, during the night of a full moon (to encourage romantic love or love's fullness). The next day, sprinkle a bit into both of your shoes so love walks with you. Sprinkle the rest on the walkway leading to your house so love follows you home.

Love Juice

When you think of philtres or love potions, you might imagine a Witch standing over a large, cast-iron cauldron brewing a foul-smelling concoction and chanting incantations over her heady mixture. You can still get an old-fashioned cast-iron Witch's cauldron for making love potions, but more often than not, today's cauldrons take the shape of blenders, juicers, and food processors. Make and drink this delicious love potion to put a little more love and passion into your life. You will need six red apples, four ripe pears, and a tiny piece of fresh ginger (optional). Remove the core and seeds from the apples and pears. Cut the fruit into small pieces and put the pieces through the juicer along with the ginger. As you juice the ingredients, focus your awareness on putting love into them.

The key to empowering potions is to stay focused on your magickal goal for the entire time it takes to make and use the potion. Pour the potion into a glass, hold it in your hands, and say,

> Move loving, more caring
>
> More passion, more sharing
>
> As I will, so be it!

Sip the potion with your lover and, as you do, imagine more love and passion flowing into your relationship.

Candle Enchantment

Get a red candle and carve a heart into it about halfway down. If you wish, also dress the candle with love oil (rose or vanilla), moving from the bottom up to build energy. Every night from the waxing to full moon, light the candle for a few minutes and say,

> Wishes in this candle, red
>
> Heed these words as they're said.
>
> I wish for a relationship of the heart,
>
> Here, tonight, the Love Magick starts.

On the night of the full moon let the candle burn past the heart emblem, then either call some friends to go out or perhaps join a singles chat room online and see who you meet. This spell usually manifests within one cycle (a week, month, or year of casting). If you like, you can repeat it every moon cycle until you meet your love.

Luck

Being lucky doesn't solve every problem in life, but it sure helps! Generally speaking, use luck spells to tip the scales in your favor, and when you need just a little extra edge in a situation that you wouldn't have normally. Whether you are in Vegas for the weekend, desperately trying to undelete a file from your computer's backup files, or trying to put together the latest toy for your child (and there isn't an 8-year-old handy), a little luck can really count. Luck (plus actually reading the instructions) can also help you when you are trying to hook up the latest techno-gadget to your computer, TV, or stereo.

Pennies From Heaven

Take a penny from your pocket and put it on a scrap of green paper or a piece of paper in your lucky color. Draw the outline of the penny several times all over the paper and a large sun at the top (representing the heavens). Fold this inward on itself three times for easy carrying. Hold the token in your hands and say,

> Lady luck be my guide,
>
> Lady luck stand by my side.

Keep this token in your pocket (at your side) when you need luck the most.

Lucky Fortune Cookie

Next time you get a fortune in a fortune cookie that you really like, keep and use it to bring more luck into your life. Hold the fortune in your power hand, read it out loud, and then say three times,

> May good fortune come my way
>
> Make this my lucky day!

For the next three weeks, take a minute every day to hold the fortune in your hand, read it out loud, and repeat the incantation. Carry the fortune with you, in your purse, wallet, or safely in your pocket to encourage good luck.

Mechanical Maintenance

We have friends who seem to have proverbial mechanical curses. It doesn't matter if it's a car, TV, or toaster, these items are always in need of repair. If you know someone like this, you may want to share some of these spells with her or him. Also try them yourself to keep the amount of mechanical mayhem in your house down to a minimum.

Tool-Kit Correction

Every home has some spot where tools gather, be it a drawer or a formalized kit. This spell is designed to fill that area with supportive and protective energy. The idea here is that (a) those tools will then function more effectively when you use them, and (b) because you're protecting them hopefully they won't be needed as much! For this spell, take one whole bud of garlic (to keep away all sorts of nasty stuff) and wrap it in white cloth. Hold the garlic and cloth in your power hand and say,

> Breakdowns and losses are the homeowners bane,
>
> So I empower you my tools to maintain!

Put the cloth-covered garlic bud into the kit or drawer where your most commonly utilized tools get stored to keep them in good working order.

Who You Gonna Call?

To keep the ghosts out of your machines, try this blessing and protection spell. Call in the Watchtowers and draw a Magick Circle. If possible, take the machine into the Circle. If it's too large, draw the Circle around the machine. Next, place your hands on the machine. If it's small enough, hold it between your hands. Face or look Northward, and say,

> I call upon the Cyber Spirits of Earth
>
> And ask them to bless and protect this machine
>
> And keep it from malfunctioning.

Face or look Eastward, and say,

> I call upon the Cyber Spirits of Air
>
> And ask them to bless and protect this machine
>
> And keep it from malfunctioning.

Face or look Southward, and say,

> I call upon the Cyber Spirits of Fire
>
> And ask them to bless and protect this machine
>
> And keep it from malfunctioning.

Face or look Westward, and say,

> I call upon the Cyber Spirits of Water
>
> And ask them to bless and protect this machine
>
> And keep it from malfunctioning.

Your machine is now blessed and protected.

Money

The Cyber Witch often craves the ultimate gadgets with which to weave his or her spells. Unfortunately, we don't all have the budget to keep up with the ever-transforming face of technology. That's where money spells come in handy. Use them to improve financial flow, balance the budgets, safeguard your savings, and generally provide you with a better sense of where your money goes so that you can direct it more effectively. Just bear in mind that this isn't about "getting rich quick." The universe will expect you to do your part here (such as by working harder so you can get that raise!)

Give to Receive

The universe has built in checks and balances. Trish has often found that when she's in dire need of money, giving up something special often opens the way for that providence. To try this yourself, you need to pick out something that has special meaning to you (in other words, it's hard to give up). Either sell this item or give it to someone you know has a need of it. Usually within a week of the gift or the sale, money follows threefold.

Wallet Wealth

To keep your money and credit cards where they belong (in your wallet), try this little spell. Take an alfalfa sprout and adhere it to a piece of tape or inside a snippet of waxed paper (so it "sticks"). Alfalfa is a symbol of providence. Put this into your wallet down deep in the fold and say,

> Help me with my spending ways,
>
> Where this rests my money stays!

The Color of Money

The natural harmonic energies of color, a powerful visual component in magick, can greatly enhance your spellcrafting. For this spell, you'll need a green candle, a green flashlight, and a dollar bill. The color green sets the stage for prosperity and wealth. First, light the candle and say,

> Candle of money, flame of prosperity,
>
> Bring fortune and wealth to me.
>
> Blessed be! So shall it be!

Then turn on the flashlight, point it in all directions, North, East, South, and West (in that order). Say,

> Lamp of money, light of prosperity
>
> Bring fortune and wealth to me.
>
> Blessed be! So shall it be!

Next, fold the dollar bill three times, and then carefully drip a three drops of candle wax on the bill. Say,

> Three times three times three
>
> Bring me money and prosperity.
>
> Blessed be! So shall it be!

Keep the dollar bill in your wallet or purse to bring you more money.

Negativity

Even the most upbeat of Cyber Witches has "down" days when nothing seems to go right. Additionally, those who live in urban environments are bombarded with negative vibes from thousands of sources. This means that the wise Witch keeps a few negativity spells in her handy magickal knapsack.

Keep it Clean

To rid yourself of negativity or just to unwind, take advantage of modern plumbing and immerse yourself in a ritual bath or, better yet, the techno-cauldron of the Goddess, the hot tub. Crush three bay leaves and put them into a cup of boiling water. Steep for about 15 minutes, strain the leaves out, and pour the water into a warm bath. (Note: If you are using a hot tub for this spell, use nine bay leaves.) Close your eyes and relax in the bay leaf bath for at least 10 minutes. Imagine the water washing all the negativity out of your body, mind, and spirit. If your mind wanders, just bring your focus back to letting go of all that built up negativity inside of you. Say to yourself three times,

> Wash away negativity
>
> Soak in positivity.

When you are done soaking, dry off with a super soft cotton towel. If you have a towel-heating rack, put it to use here! As you are toweling off, imagine completely wiping away any residual negativity with the towel. Be sure to wash the towel before using it again.

Smoke 'Em Out

Rid your space or focals of negativity by smudging. You'll need a sage and cedar smudging wand, which you can purchase at health food stores, Witch shops, or over the Internet. Or you can make your own wand by tieing up dried sage and cedar into a wand. A candle flame works the best for lighting smudge. As soon as the wand starts to smolder, turn on a fan (in warmer weather) or a heater (in cooler weather), and blow the smudge smoke in every direction and over your focals. Make sure the space is well ventilated to avoid setting off the smoke detector, although this can add to the power of the spell by scaring off those nasty energies. Hold the burning wand over a fireproof bowl or dish as the burning herbs might drop off. As you smudge, say,

> Spirits of North, East, West, and South
>
> With this smoke, bless and protect this space (or focal),
>
> Now completely rid it of any negativity.
>
> Blessed be! As I will, so shall it be!

When you finish smudging the area and/or focal, smudge yourself by allowing the fan or heater to blow the smudge smoke over your body. When you are done, put the smudge wand in water to extinguish it. Turn the fan or heater off.

Note: For a smokeless alternative to smudge, use sage and cedar oil in an aromatherapy diffuser.

Opportunity

There are moments in everyone's life when opportunity knocks, but no one is home to answer the door! Sometimes we need to give opportunity a helping hand by weaving our magick in such a way as to bring those chances to us at the right place and the right time.

Three Times Is a Charm

This spell was inspired by Sirona's son. He always points out whenever the clock is showing triple numbers, which he calls magick numbers. For example, 1:11, 2:22, 3:33, 4:44, and 5:55 are all magick numbers, with the master magick number being 11:11. For this spell, we are going to use the magick three number because three is a sacred number of the Triple Goddess, and nine (3+3+3) is the master number of the Ninefold Goddess. Whenever you see a digital clock showing 3:33, use the magick three number to bring you opportunity. First, quickly ask your favorite Goddess to help empower you (you only have a minute to do this spell before the clock changes). Then say,

> Magick three, three, three
>
> Now bring me opportunity.
>
> By the Lady, blessed be!

Do this every time you see the magick three number, whether at home, at work, or when visiting, shopping, or driving in your car. The more you do it, the more opportunities you will have.

Note: Use the magick 2:22 number to bring more co-operation at home or 1:11 to start new projects. Just match the numbers to the magick!

Brewing Opportunity

The coffee maker makes the perfect cauldron for your morning ritual potion of a cup of hot java because it combines all four Elements in one techno-tool: Earth (pot, machine, and coffee beans), Air (pungent aroma), Fire (power on and heating device), Water (the water and coffee) and Spirit (you drinking the coffee). When you are making your coffee in the morning, say a short blessing, such as,

> Bless this cup of coffee
>
> Impart its power into me.
>
> By the Lady, blessed be!

When the coffee is brewed, whisper a short prayer into the coffee before drinking it. Whisper,

> Dear Goddess, I pray today
>
> That opportunities will come my way.

Overcoming

What stands between you and living a successful, fulfilled life? What habits or problems would you like to banish? Overcoming spells are designed to handle both sides of this equation. They can build a bridge to your goals and also help you with those that don't work for you.

Wash My Troubles Away

Using non-toxic washable ink or washable paint, write down the things that are most troubling you on a garment such as an old T-shirt, pants, or nightgown. To simplify the process, use one word statements, names, and so forth, for example, "debt" or "fear." Pour liquid laundry detergent directly on top of the words, and then put the garment in the washing machine by itself, without other clothes. Turn on the washing machine. When the wash cycle is complete, take the shirt out. See that your troubles have been all washed away. You can repeat this spell as often as you like. It's great fun (writing on their clothes) for kids to get rid of their problems this way too!

Cutting the Cord

You'll need a three-foot piece of wire or electrical cord and a pair of wire cutters for this spell. You won't be able to use the cord again, so something such as a frayed extension cord is ideal. Hold the cord in your hands and begin knotting it. As you knot it, focus on putting the problem you want to overcome into the knot. You are literally tieing the problem into the electrical cord or wire. Do this nine times. With each knot you make, say,

> I tie this problem into this wire
>
> I overcome the muck and mire!

When you are done knotting the wire, take the wire cutters and carefully cut the cord into nine pieces. As you cut the cord, imagine that you are cutting all your troubles out of your life—as if you are slicing right through them. With each cut you make, say,

> With each cut of this sword
>
> I cut my problems from this cord.

After you are done cutting the cord into nine pieces, put the pieces in a bag. Pour salt into the bag, about halfway, on top of the cord pieces, and then put the bag into the garbage.

Peace

Peace within is a powerful coping mechanism for today's hectic pace. And manifesting that peace without—personally and globally—is even more powerful! Spells for peace begin within because we must have that inner harmony before we can hope to help the world come to terms with its issues.

Paradise Potion

Avalon, the land of the apples, is the Celtic paradise. This potion uses the healing powers of the apple to create a more peaceful feeling. Gather together two cups of seedless grapes, three apples, and nine strawberries. Charge them with your intention (to be more peaceful and less stressed-out). Then core the apples and remove the seeds. Trim the strawberries and grapes, and cut the apples into small pieces. Put the grapes and strawberries in the juicer, and then add the apples. As you put the fruit into the juicer, be sure to charge it, using your touch as well as focusing on your magick goal. Next, add pure water to the mixture to thin as desired. Hold the potion in your hands, and say a blessing over it:

> Helpful Cyber Spirits
>
> Of space, Earth, sky, and sea
>
> Bless this fruit-filled potion
>
> By the Lady, blessed be!

Drink the paradise potion to uplift your spirits and feel more at ease with yourself and the world.

Virtual Beach Vacation

Most of us could use a vacation from the daily grind, but we don't have the time or money to go on a really blissful vacation. This cyber visualization takes you on just such a vacation, and all you need are your computer screen and your imagination. You don't even need to bring your toothbrush!

First, pull up a graphic of a beautiful beach with palm trees, miles of warm, soft sand, and deep blue waters. Type in "tropical beach" or "island beaches," for example, and then click on the graphic and save it as a GIF or JPEG file. Sit or recline in front of the screen with the beach graphic, and gaze at it for a couple of minutes. Next, close your eyes and take a few deep breaths, letting any tensions flow out of you as you exhale. Now relax your body by flexing your muscles (in your feet, legs, hips, stomach, neck, arms, and hands) as tight as you can, and then let them go limp. Imagine white light filling your body. Open your eyes and look at the beach graphic on your screen. Imprint it in you mind. Then close your eyes and imagine yourself on that very beach—peacefully sitting under the palm tree, feeling the warm breeze against your face and the warmth of the sand on your feet. Imagine digging your feet into the warm sand and feeling it between your toes. Dip your feet into the warm blue ocean water. Smell the salt in the air, and then taste the salt on your lips from the mist off the water. Allow yourself to feel peaceful and calm. Keep referring to the graphic on the screen to go deeper into the experience. Enjoy your mini-vacation at the virtual beach for at least 15 minutes. When you are done, exit the screen. Any time you need to feel more peaceful and calm, just pull up the virtual beach graphic, kick back, and enjoy another mini-vacation.

Note: If you have a color printer, you can print out the graphic, and carry it with you wherever you go.

Protection

The world is not the safe haven it was at the turn of the 20th century. People cannot leave doors unlocked or children unattended without fear. We, as would many people, would like to see a safer and kinder world. The Cyber Witch, being proactive in his or her approach to life, thinks about both the beauties and dangers of modern living. Protection magick is intended to ward off trouble *before* it happens.

Disk Guardians

You can make guardians for your Circle, cyber and otherwise, using four floppy disks. First, erase the disks, and smudge them in cedar and sage smudge or sandalwood incense. Next, download information and graphics onto each one. Be sure to match the information and graphics with the direction they represent—North/Earth, East/Air, South/Fire, and West/Water.

Colored disks work great because you can match the color to the direction (green or black for North, yellow for East, red for South, and blue for West). You can paint magickal symbols on them; add stickers; glue on glitter, small crystals, leaves, cedar and pine needles, acorns, and seashells; tie them with colored ribbon, and so forth. Remember to smudge your decorative items before affixing them to the disks to rid them of any unwanted energies. Once again, match the decoration with the direction the disk represents. Charge your disk guardians with the appropriate elemental power—Earth, Air, Fire, or Water. Then, set them at the four points of your Sacred Circle to stand guard and watch over your magick making and rituals.

Power Animal Speak

Many a tale begins with the line, "These things happened long ago, when animals could speak like humans." In folklore, animals are reincarnated ancestors, divine messengers, supernatural beings, creators, familiars, and supporters of the world—most of whom could talk just as people could. This isn't all that much of a stretch, considering that today talking animals are common in cartoons, in movies, and in animated e-cards on the Internet. You can tap into animal power to protect yourself and your family, workplace, and home. First, select a talking stuffed animal to be your cyber power animal. For example, there are singing and dancing reindeer, bears, and wolves, as well as remote control woolly mammoths, robotic dogs, cats, birds, and bugs. If you have children, you probably have a few of these animals already around the house. If not, you can find one at most department stores or on the Internet. Select the animal with which you feel the strongest connection, and then put the toy animal in a prominent place in your home, workplace, or car to bring in its protective powers.

Technological glitches

No one wants his or her cell phone battery to die or their computer connection to fail at the absolutely wrong moment. Of course, this is usually exactly when such things occur. These charms and spells are designed to help avert computer crashes, DVD disasters, and video violations:

Bug Off

Use this spell to protect dozens of your technological items. It's very simple. Find a large bay leaf and inscribe the rune of protection on it (it looks a bit like a capital Y). Repeat this incantation eight times for completion:

> Keep glitches, malfunctions, and all bugs away,
>
> By my will and the power of bay!

Take the bay leaf and seal it inside a small piece of waxed paper (use an iron on low setting). This keeps the leaf from crumbling. Now put it wherever you need it—under the phone, under your tower, near the VCR, and so forth.

A Rune With a View

You can use runes to minimize those technological glitches and protect your machines. Use a clean soft towel to trace the runes of Berkana (for the Goddess), Ansuz (for Odin), Uruz (for strength), Algiz (for divine protection), and Ingwaz (designates the four Quarters of the Sacred Circle) on your techno-tools such as your TV, dishwater, blender, coffee grinder, and lawn tractor. As you trace the runes on the item with the towel, say,

> Runes of wisdom, runes of light
>
> Protect this *(name of item)* with all your might.

Unwanted wights, wend away

Helpful spirits, stay!

Travel

We live in a highly mobile society, and many Cyber Witches spend hundreds of hours on the road, in the air, and just generally getting from here to there. We'd like to do so safely, so we surround ourselves with various forms of protective magick. From speeding tickets to traffic jams, here are a few examples of how to safeguard yourself from the normal hazards of travel:

Car Altars

Although designed specifically for automobiles, this little item packs nicely into a backpack, suitcase, purse, or brief-case. If you like, you can even hang one off your broom! You'll need a small cloth approximately 4 × 4. Any color or fabric will do, but try to choose something sturdy and a color that represents safety to you. Into the center of that cloth place a stone (Earth), a small feather (Air), a match (Fire), and a small seashell (Water). If possible also include the ashes from a sacred fire. Bundle the whole thing up with a white ribbon and say,

String of white wrapped firmly round,

Within this bundle my magick's bound.

No matter where I may roam,

Bring me safely back to home.

Make several of these to put in small places, such as the glove compartment in your car. By the way, if you have a real emergency, open the bundle and release the contents for faster manifestation.

Nature Power

Cars, trucks, vans, buses, trains, helicopters, and airplanes are our mechanical horses, oxen, llamas, mules, donkeys, and elephants. In regards to your car, ideally it represents your own self, in terms of travel and transportation. Your automobile may also represent your power animal, for example, cars are named "mustang," "thunderbird," and "ram." To protect your car, truck, or van and yourself when traveling in it, put a power animal in it, in toy form, to remind you of Nature's inherent power. For example, Sirona uses a toy beagle whose head bobs up and down because beagles are one of her power animals. If you are lucky enough to have a pet that likes to travel with you in your vehicle, she or he will act as a natural guardian when you are traveling. Remember to never leave your pet companions in car by themselves when it's hot or freezing outside.

Wishes

Wishing is among the oldest forms of spellcraft. Our ancestors tossed coins in a well, cast their hopes out to the first star appearing at night, and blew out birthday candles even as we do to this day. These traditions have a great deal of value, but how does the not-so-traditional Cyber Witch wish? Here are a few ideas for doing just that.

Search-Engine Spellcraft

Search engines enable you to do virtual window shopping—and the best thing is you don't have to dress up, put your face on, or spend a penny if you don't want to. Here's how it works. During your surfing times, pay attention to items or images that represent a personal wish in literal or symbolic form. Save those images in a favorites folder marked "manifestation." As you save each image, say,

Cyber Spirits so bright

I wish I may, I wish I might

Manifest this wish into my life.

As I will, so shall it be!

That way every time you open an item in that folder, you also open the way for that wish to begin taking form in reality!

Watt's Your Wish?

Rubbing a magick lamp with a genie inside releases the powerful helper, plus it gives you three magick wishes. You'll need a lamp (a symbol of hope) and a soft cloth (fabric of life) for this lamp wishing spell. Any lamp will do. First, turn on the lamp. Then slowly and deliberately rub the body of the lamp with the cloth, using clockwise strokes. The sunwise (clockwise) motion engenders positive solar energy. As you do this, focus on three special wishes, one at a time. Use the slow, rhythmic movements of the cloth to strengthen your focus. Keep rubbing for at least 15 minutes. Every time you turn on the lamp, you activate the wish energy and increase the probability of your wishes coming true.

Barbecue Blessing

Our ancestors often sent their prayers and other requests to the heavens via the smoke of a sacred Fire. Now, being a pragmatic Cyber Witch, you're going to combine this idea with dinner! Pick out a food that represents your wish and prepare it with suitable herbs. For example, when Trish feels tender love has been wanting in her home, she makes marinated strawberry chicken. The marinade softens hearts, the strawberry is for love, and the chicken for healing. Sirona, being a vegetarian, likes to grill all kinds of vegetables, basted with Thai honey butter sauce, when she wants to sweeten things up.

As your meal cooks, whisper your wishes into the resulting smoke, which takes that desire upward and out to the four corners of creation.

Eat expectantly and enjoy!

Bibliography

Baumgartner, Anne. *A Comprehensive Dictionary of the Gods*. New York: University Books, 1984.

Bowes, Susan. *Notions and Potions*. New York: Sterling Publishing Co., Inc., 1997.

Farrar, Janet and Stewart. *The Witches' Way*. London: Robert Hale, 1984.

Grimassi, Raven. *The Wiccan Mysteries*. St. Paul, Minn.: Llewellyn Publications, 1997.

Gray, Deborah. *The Good Witch's Guide to Wicked Ways*. Boston: Journey Editions, 2001.

Green, Miranda J. *Dictionary of Celtic Myth and Legend*. New York: Thames and Hudson, 1997.

Grimal, Pierre, ed. *Larousse World Mythology*. London: Paul Hamlyn, 1965.

Heath, Maya. *Cerridwen's Handbook of Incense, Oils, and Candles*. San Antonio, Texas: Words of Wizdom International, Inc., 1996.

Johnson, Cait. *Witch in the Kitchen*. Rochester, Vt.: Destiny Books, 2001.

Jung, Carl G. *The Archetypes of the Collective Unconscious*. Princeton, N.J.: Princeton University Press, 1990.

Knight, Sirona. *A Witch Like Me*. Franklin Lakes, N.J.: New Page Books, 2001.

———. *Celtic Traditions*. New York: Citadel Press, 2000.

———. *Dream Magic: Night Spells and Rituals For Love, Prosperity, and Personal Power*. San Francisco: HarperSanFrancisco, 2000.

———. *Exploring Celtic Druidism*. Franklin Lakes, N.J.: New Page Books, 2001.

———. *The Little Giant Encyclopedia of Runes*. New York: Sterling Publishing Co., 2000.

———. *Love, Sex, and Magick*. New York: Citadel Press, 1999.

———. *The Pocket Guide to Celtic Spirituality*. Freedom, Calif.: Crossing Press, 1998.

———. *The Pocket Guide to Crystals and Gemstones*. Freedom, Calif.: Crossing Press, 1998.

———. *The Wiccan Spell Kit*. New York: Kensington Books, 2001.

———. *The Witch and Wizard Training Guide*. New York: Kensington Books, 2001.

Knight, Sirona, et al. *The Shapeshifter Tarot*. St. Paul, Minn.: Llewellyn Publications, 1998.

Leach, Maria, ed. *Standard Dictionary of Folklore, Mythology, and Legend*. New York: Funk & Wagnalls Co., 1950.

Linn, Denise. *The Secret Language of Signs*. New York: Ballantine Book, 1996.

Monaghan, Patricia. *The Book of Goddesses and Heroines.* St. Paul, Minn.: Llewellyn Publications, 1990.

Rector-Page, Linda. *Healthy Healing.* Sonona, Calif.: Healthy Healing Publications, 1992.

Squire, Charles. *Celtic Myth and Legend.* Franklin Lakes, N.J.: New Page Books, 2001.

Stewart, R. J. *Celtic Gods, Celtic Goddesses.* New York: Sterling Publishing Co., 1990.

Telesco, Patricia. *A Charmed Life.* Franklin Lakes, N.J.: New Page Books, 2000.

———. *A Witch's Beverages and Brews.* Franklin Lakes, N.J.: New Page Books, 2001.

———. *Advanced Wicca.* Secaucus, N.J.: Citadel Press, 1999.

———. *Goddess in My Pocket.* San Francisco: HarperCollins San Francisco, 1998.

———. *The Herbal Arts.* Secaucus, N.J.: Citadel Press, 1998.

———. *The Little Book of Love Magic.* Freedom, Calif.: Crossing Press, 1999.

———. *Magic Made Easy.* San Francisco: HarperCollins San Francisco, 1999.

———. *Spinning Spells, Weaving Wonders.* Freedom, Calif.: Crossing Press, Inc., 1996.

———. *Wishing Well.* Freedom, Calif.: Crossing Press, Inc., 1997.

Telesco, Patricia, and Sirona Knight. *The Wiccan Web.* New York: Citadel Press, 2001.

Worwood, Valerie. *The Complete Book of Essential Oils and Aromatherapy.* New York: New World Library, 1995.

Index

About the Authors

Sirona Knight is the author of 13 books on magick, Wicca, and the Goddess, including *A Witch Like Me, Exploring Celtic Druidism,* and *Faery Magick.* She has been a contributing editor for *Magical Blend* magazine for more than six years. Sirona also has a master's degree in stress management from California State University. She lives in the woods of Northern California near Chico, California. For more information, visit her Web site, *www.sironaknight.com.*

Trish Telesco is a mother of three, wife, chief human to five pets, and full-time professional author with numerous metaphysical books on the market. These include *Goddess in My Pocket, The Herbal Arts, Kitchen Witch's Cookbook, The Little Book of Love Magic, Your Book of Shadows, A Charmed Life, Spinning Spells, Weaving Wonders,* and other diverse titles, each of which represents a different area of spiritual interest.

Trish considers herself a down-to-earth, wooden spoon-wielding Kitchen Witch whose love of folklore and worldwide customs flavor every spell and ritual. Although her

Wiccan education was originally self-trained and self-initiated, she later received initiation into the Strega tradition of Italy, which gives form and fullness to the folk magick Trish practices. Her strongest beliefs lie in following personal vision: being tolerant of other traditions, making life an act of worship, and being creative so that magic grows with you.

Trish travels minimally twice a month to give lectures and workshops around the country. She has appeared on several television segments, including one for *Sightings* on multicultural divination systems. Besides this, Trish maintains a strong visible presence on the Internet through popular sites such as:

❊ *witchvox.com* (festival focus),

❊ *loresinger.com* (her Web site),

❊ *groups.yahoo.com/group/folkmagicwithtrishtelesco/* (her Yahoo club),

and various other appearances on Internet chats and bbs boards.

Her hobbies include fire circle dancing, drumming, gardening, herbalism, brewing, singing, handcrafts, antique restoration, and landscaping. Her current project is helping support Pagan land funds.